He opened the pi____ her. She wished he w____ very well what his smile did to most women. Not her, of course, but most women. "It's never hard on a man's ego when a woman thinks he'd be good in the sack."

Rita rolled her eyes. "Well, it was the drugs talking, not Mom."

"You think so?" Instead of getting in the rig, he strode toward her and put his hands on her waist.

She gazed into his eyes, darker in the evening light. "I know so. I've never heard her say such things." She knew she should pull out of his grasp, but somehow her body didn't obey her mind.

"Doesn't mean she wasn't telling her real thoughts." His face drew nearer hers.

"Don't believe what she said about how I feel about you." Her voice breathless, she knew she should escape, but somehow she couldn't.

"No?" His hands tightened on her waist and his eyes darkened.

She held still, hoping he wouldn't kiss her, but not able to resist staring at his lips. "Lord, help me."

To Dee + Sam!

Down Home Ever Lovin' Mule Blues

Jacquie Rogers

So nice to meet you!
Don't spit up wind. ☺

Highland Press Publishing
Florida

Jacquie Rogers

Down Home Everlovin' Mule Blues

For information, please contact
Highland Press Publishing,
PO Box 2292, High Springs, FL 32655.
www.highlandpress.org

ISBN: 978-0-9800356-8-1

HIGHLAND PRESS PUBLISHING

Western Imprint

Dedication

To my brother, Ken Walker, who has stuck by me through thick and thin. Please don't anyone tell him, but he's the best brother a girl could ever ask for.
Special thanks to Angie Butterworth, Ann Charles, Eilis Flynn, Sherrie Holmes, Judith Laik, Wendy Linstad, Mary Alice Meirz, Nancy Radke, Gerri Russell, Leanne Shawler, and Sherry Walker. Lots of people read this book and helped me make it better.

Many thanks also to my editor, Leanne Burroughs who had confidence in this mule, er story, and to cover designer, Deborah Macgillivray. I love this cover! And so does Socrates, which is saying something. Extra special thanks to Deborah for going above and beyond the call of duty and working on my cover when she has her own deadlines looming. Of course, Socrates wouldn't have it any other way.

And always, my real life hero is Mark.

Acknowledgements

Two men had a lot to do with the forming of Brody Alexander's character. One was a former bullrider who wrote *A Cowboy Never Lies*, and *A Cowboy Never Lies 2*, the late Dan Burnett. We met when I interviewed him for our local writers' group newsletter. His humor and, well, bullheadedness, played strongly in Brody's makeup.

The man who explained how bulls move and think, and who talked at length about bullfighting techniques was former rodeo clown and bullfighter, Jim O'Keefe. I thank Jim for his infinite patience and explaining things over again until I understood. He also talked me through a whole show, how he used his acts, the attitudes of a clown, and how his mindset changes the instant a bull comes into the arena. He talked about cowboy protection, techniques, and risks. From him, I learned about the frequent and often serious injuries, and how bullfighters continue the show despite the pain, because the riders' safety is their responsibility. Thank you, Jim.

Rodeo people are a different breed—an incredible bunch of people who are stalwart in their beliefs and honorable in their hearts. But they're a little bit crazy, and that's what this book is about. As Dan would say, "May your saddle never slip."

Chapter 1

Grasmere, Idaho

Humans are so stubborn.
But never let it be said that we mules don't take care of our humans. Mine is Brody Alexander. I'm Socrates, master of cogitation and entertainer of both large and small children.
Infinite patience is required to endure Brody's obstinance. Granted, we john mules do have it easier than men. We don't have this hormone thing going on so we don't spend our lives trying to make little mules.
That gives us lots more time to cogitate. And believe me, I can think of a few more species who could do with a little thoughtful uncommon sense.
Human males, for instance. Why, they seem to spend every waking hour thinking about sex, getting sex, or being disappointed by not having sex.
That's how I see it. Except I left one thing out—human males need more than sex. They need love. My human could use a little loving these days. Why, he's been moping around worse than a porcupine on a bad hair day.
That's where the cogitating comes in. If testosterone hadn't clouded Brody's thinking, he'd already know what he needs. Funny thing, those hormones.
The way I see it, my job is to help his brain listen to his other parts—especially his heart. And I have the answer. Yes, sir, I do. I just saw a pretty little filly drive down the road, the very same one who mooned over Brody ten years ago.

It's time for action.

Brody Alexander stomped into the house and threw his battered Stetson on the table. "Luke, have you seen that dang mule? He's let himself out of the barn again."

Luke smashed his cigarette in the ashtray. "Nope, but I s'pose he'll show up once he gets a little hungry. Or cold. Old Socrates don't like the cold." Luke slurped his coffee and let out a satisfied sigh. "There's scrambled eggs on the stove."

The phone rang. He nodded toward it. "That might be him now."

"Don't be a smart ass." Brody yanked the handset off the cradle. "Hello."

"Howdy. Your mule's in our pantry eating apples." He recognized the partly annoyed, partly amused voice of Judy Markum, the middle-aged widow from up the road.

"Uh, sorry, ma'am. I'll be right over."

Luke chuckled. "It was him, wasn't it?"

"Smart ass." Grabbing his hat, Brody made for the pickup and hitched up the trailer—the splint on his left arm not making the task any easier, or his humor any better. Sometimes he'd like to kick that dang mule into next Sunday.

Perseus, his Australian Shepherd, hopped into the pickup before Brody had the door halfway open. The old '62 Chevy was already warmed up from hauling feed to the cattle. The heater worked even if the rest of the pickup decided not to—a blessing in the crisp autumn Owyhee mornings. He took off for the Markum place.

Five minutes of bumpy dirt road later, he pulled in front of Judy's white stucco house with yellow trim. Snapdragons and petunias grew along the perimeter of the house, and the tinkle of the wind chimes seemed to smile on visitors.

She stood in the front doorway propped on her crutches, waving him in. At least she had a smile on her weathered face. He got out of the pickup and tipped his hat at her.

"Good morning, Judy."

Her dog, Beauty, ran up and nuzzled his hand. He obliged her with a few quick scratches behind her ears. A late-model tan Volvo was parked beside the Markum barn. He smirked, knowing that no local would have an expensive, foreign car with no ground clearance. Socrates had picked a mighty poor time to work up a hunger for the neighbor's apples.

"Come on in, Brody." Judy seemed quite happy for a woman with a mule in her house.

He took off his hat and trudged in. "Evenin', ma'am. I'm sorry about Socrates. Where is he? I'll get him out of your hair."

"It's my apples I'm worried about, not my hair." She pointed to a curtained room off the kitchen. "He's in there. Probably the happiest miniature mule in the world right now."

Brody made for the pantry, ready to give that mule the what-for. But the obnoxious beast beat him to the punch, sauntering out with a Red Delicious in his mouth. Socrates dodged Brody's one-handed grab for the halter and trotted into the living room.

Brody gritted his teeth. Judy's guests would be in there, and here he had to chase a flea-bitten mule. Oh well, might as well act the clown. After all, he did it for a living.

"I do *not* want that animal on my new carpet!" Judy hobbled after him.

He held her back and called to the mule, "Socrates, get your tush out here." In two long strides, Brody managed to grab the mule's halter. "What in the Sam Hill do you think you're doing? Let's go home."

"Hello, cowboy." The feminine voice was sultry, and familiar.

Brody stopped cold, took a breath, and turned toward the voice.

There she sat on the couch, little Rita Markum, holding the apple Socrates had brought her. Only she wasn't little anymore. Not that she'd grown taller or gotten fat. Nope, she'd filled out into one helluva woman. He felt a certain amount of compassion for old Adam in the Garden of Eden. If Eve bore any resemblance to Rita, poor Adam never had a chance.

He couldn't help but notice the tasteful tan linen business suit she wore—and the smooth, shapely thigh exposed when she crossed her legs. Brody's mouth went dry. Whew, baby. Her hair was still blonde, although shorter, and her blue eyes even bluer. He hoped she still wanted him like she did that day of her high school graduation, because he sure wouldn't mind taking up where they left off.

"Brody Alexander, if you don't get that infernal animal off my carpet, I'm going to beat you both!" Judy stood behind him with a crutch raised, ready to inflict bodily damage.

"Yes, ma'am." He tugged on the halter, but Socrates wouldn't budge. Brody swore under his breath—on account of ladies being present.

"After you get that stubborn mule trailered," Judy said, "come back in and I'll make some coffee. I baked cookies yesterday."

He stole one more glance at Rita. The mule took a step and Brody thanked the Good Lord above.

He wished he could stay, but Luke had already fixed breakfast and wouldn't be too amused if Brody didn't eat his cooking. "I'm sorry, I've got to get back to my morning chores." His stomach growled.

The mule put on his brakes, leaning back on his hind legs and stiffening his front legs. Brody pulled and yanked, but old Socrates wouldn't budge an inch.

Rita arched an eyebrow and folded her arms beneath her bosom. "Looks like you're working up an appetite."

Such a sweet bosom, too. He didn't remember her being so well endowed. But he could mull the matter later. Right now, he needed to get this ornery mule out of the house before Judy clobbered him. It looked like he was going to have to pick up all three hundred pounds of the stubborn creature and carry him out of there. "Yes, ma'am."

Socrates took a step, and Brody was glad to get out before he made a total ass of himself. "But I do have to get going." The mule stopped again. Brody pulled harder, but the mule wouldn't budge.

"I doubt that. It's eight-thirty," Judy said. "You should have all your chores done by now."

Maybe coffee and cookies would hit the spot. He sneaked another glance at Rita's bosom. The scenery wouldn't hurt his digestion any, either. "I'll be right back, as soon as I can convince this apple thief to go outside."

Socrates bolted toward the door and nearly jerked Brody's arm out of its socket in the process. The suddenly frisky mule made the trip through the kitchen downright perilous as Brody had to hop over a kitchen chair, then barely miss getting his nose plastered all over the door frame, but he refused to let go of the lead rope. He opened the trailer gate and the mule hopped in, pretty as you please. Brody shook his head, wondering what in tarnation had gotten into the old boy.

By the time he'd returned to the kitchen, Judy sat at the table while Rita poured three cups of coffee. A plate piled high with homemade chocolate chippers looked mighty inviting. And a cookie or two certainly wouldn't spoil his appetite for Luke's dried-up scrambled eggs.

Judy motioned to the chair opposite her and Brody sat in it.

"I guess you and Rita will have to get reacquainted. You two have come and gone over the last few years—I don't imagine you've seen each other for quite some time."

Brody tipped his hat at Judy's daughter, then remembered his hat was still on in the house, for Pete's sake. He whipped it off and ran his fingers through his hair for good measure. "Howdy," he said, smiling his most charming smile.

She smiled back—a faint one, but she smiled, nonetheless— and placed a cup of coffee in front of him. "Almost ten years."

He nodded his thanks, wondering what to say to her. He'd known her when she wore painted-on pants and ran for rodeo queen at the local rodeos. And he'd turned her down flat when she wanted to find out what lovin' was all about. Heck, she had been jailbait then. But she was a full-grown beauty now.

And fair game.

"How long does it take to heal up after knee surgery?"

It took a minute for him to realize that Judy had spoken to him. Then he remembered he and Luke had offered to drive her to the hospital for her surgery in the morning.

"You've had knee surgery, right?" she asked again.

"Uh, yeah. Three times. Don't take the pain medication after three days. Flex until it hurts. Don't do anything that hurts too much until the doc gives you the go-ahead, but don't let it lie still, either. It'll seize up on you and then those damned, er, excuse my French, physical therapists will get a hold of you and turn you six ways from deliverance. Then after you heal up a bit, chuck down a pain pill and exercise the hell. . .er, heck out of it. You'll be dancing a jig in no time."

Judy took a sip of coffee. "I'm no spring chicken like you. It might take me a bit longer." He could tell she wasn't looking forward to tomorrow by the deep furrow in her usually smooth brow.

"Don't worry about it." He patted her hand. "They can fix you up good as new."

Rita sniffed. "You ought to know."

He stared at Rita, wondering why she sounded so snide. She was well aware that bullfighters got banged up all the time. Hell, he knew a guy who'd broken over a hundred bones, including his back and neck, had a steel plate in his head, and still fought bulls. In fact, he knew several men like that. Once bullfighting got into a man's blood, it stayed there.

She daintily dabbed her napkin on her lips. She hadn't eaten a thing yet, so he figured she was mindful that she'd just said a dumb thing.

"I see you still have Socrates."

"Yes, and now I have a skunk, Guinevere, and a dog, Perseus, too. I'm traveling the circuit, clowning and bullfighting. Might have to go in the can in a year or two, though."

"You don't need to say it that way," Judy protested. "It's certainly no disgrace to be a barrel man."

"Nope, but I like being in control of cowboy protection, and you can't do that from the barrel."

"I don't suppose that has anything to do with your limp or the cast on your arm." Rita placed her napkin on her lap. "Why don't you just retire?"

"Rita!" Judy glowered at her daughter. "That's not your call."

Retire? She had to be out of her mind. "I'm just a little sore, is all."

Shrugging, Rita said, "He'll end up just like Dad—stove up and dead. At least men in the city have more sense than that. David certainly does."

David? The possessive way she said his name annoyed the hell out of Brody. Who was David? Probably some jerk who counted assets on a spreadsheet all day. Poor sap. But a damned lucky sap if he'd managed to hook up with Rita. Counting her assets would be a pleasure. Brody wondered if she would've been so hostile if it hadn't been for that one sorry night when he'd had to turn her down—one of the hardest things he'd ever done. While he didn't regret it, he'd sure been sorry to see her move to the city to partake of the favors of corporate life.

And damned glad he'd made his own escape from it.

Judy took a cookie and frowned at her daughter. "So when are you going to introduce me to your fiancé?"

Fiancé? She planned to marry the sap?

"At the wedding, I suppose. He's far too busy to take time off to travel here, but I'll call him this evening and invite him to the ranch to meet you."

The scrumptious cookie turned to sawdust in Brody's mouth and he stopped chewing. So why did his gut feel like it was tied in a half-shank? He shouldn't give two hoots or a holler whether she invited her city boyfriend out here. And he didn't.

"Of course," Rita reiterated, "I'm sure he won't have time."

Judy shrugged. "It seems mighty ungentlemanly of him to marry my daughter without asking me first."

"Oh, Mom! You're so old-fashioned. Couples don't ask consent from their parents anymore."

"Old-fashioned or new-fashioned, there's such a thing as manners."

Brody scooted his chair back and stood, ready to beat a hasty retreat. He didn't mind facing down a two-thousand-pound charging bull, but he'd learned long ago not to get in the middle of a mother-daughter argument. Discussions, they called them.

"Luke and I'll be over at five in the morning to take you to the hospital. Thanks for the cookies and coffee." He nodded at them both, jammed on his hat, and made his escape.

"That won't be necessary," he heard Rita call. But he pretended not to hear. Rita would need help getting Judy home tomorrow evening whether she wanted to admit it or not. Besides, he wouldn't be able to keep Luke away with a brace of Peacemakers and a whip.

Rita stood in the doorway watching Brody drive down the road. She took a deep breath and blinked a few times to get a grip on herself. He'd taken her by surprise, he had. Her heart had skipped a beat while he'd been tussling with the four-legged apple bandit. She cursed her childhood crush on the handsome bullfighter that had stayed with her all these years.

Every girl around had had a crush on him back then. She'd wanted to lay her head on those broad shoulders of his since the day she'd first met him ten years ago. His left front tooth was just a teench crooked, making his smile all that much more engaging. And no one, absolutely no one had such a self-confident strut. The jerk.

"Rita?"

She turned to her mother, who had concern written all over her face. "Yes?"

"You can shut the door now."

"Oh." Rita stared at the door, waiting for her mother's instruction to register with her gray matter. "Of course." She pulled the door closed, then grabbed the broom propped on the kitchen wall where her mother had left it. "I'll sweep up. Socrates probably made a mess."

She shoved through the pantry curtains—away from her mother's gaze—so she could have some time to think. Picking up the few strewn apples decorated with mule tooth marks, she lamented that Brody hadn't found her attractive all those years ago. Certainly, that had to be the reason he'd turned her down. After all, his escapades with women were legendary.

She remembered him muttering some nonsense about saving her honor. Hrmmph! Lousy excuse. But if she'd had her way, she might not have such a good life now—a great job and a prestigious fiancé.

David had found her attractive, and looks were of utmost importance to him. Why he'd bought her a membership to the gym and preferred she wear dresses that made frequent visits to the gym very necessary. He enjoyed parading her in front of his friends, and she enjoyed making him happy. She also enjoyed working out, so it certainly wasn't a sacrifice.

In all honesty, though, she'd never been as drawn to David as she had been—and apparently still was—to Brody. But Brody obviously didn't share that attraction, then or now, since he could hardly wait to get away from her.

"Rita, there's not that much floor to sweep. Come on out and help me pack up for the hospital."

"Okay, Mom." She propped the broom in the corner, picked up the apples, and dumped them in the barrel before joining her mother in the kitchen. "I can't believe they're going to rebuild your knee and it's only day surgery."

"They do practically everything in day surgery now. Phyllis —you remember Phyllis at the Pie Palace—had a partial mastectomy and it was day surgery. These days they don't keep you in the hospital unless you're hooked up to an IV and about ready to croak."

"Of course I remember her. How's she doing?"

"She had breast cancer. They got it all, though, and she's doing fine now."

Judy sounded cavalier, but Rita knew deep emotions ran under that shell of understatement. "I'm glad she's okay—must've been really scary."

"Yes, we were concerned, but you know our Phyllis—can't keep her down. She only closed the diner for a few days."

Translation: the neighbors worked the diner for a week while Phyllis bossed them around. On the day and day after her chemo, a neighbor would *happen to* stop by the diner and assist. Rita knew the ways of country people. Good ways, especially the strong sense of community—truly caring for one another, was what she missed most about being away from home.

"I'll have to drop by the diner and say 'hi' to her."

"I'm sure she'd like that, but she's coming here the day after my surgery so you can visit then. You'll get to see her boy, too."

"She has a baby?"

"No, a four-year-old boy that some bucklebunny friend of hers left. But he might as well be Phyllis'—he calls her 'mom' and doesn't even remember his own."

Bucklebunnies, girls who claimed cowboys' trophy buckles in return for sexual favors, had clung to Brody since he first hit the rodeo circuit—not that he seemed to mind.

After changing clothes and catching up on the rest of the local gossip, she made a last-ditch effort to pry some funding out of MOMMI, the charitable organization associated with Pettybottham Enterprises. She'd told her mom and Phyllis that procuring funding for a children's home not under some kind of governmental aegis was futile, but still, she had to try.

"Caroline Pettybottham speaking."

"This is Rita Markham calling about the Grasmere Children's Home."

"The one with no children, no sponsor, and no license?"

"That would be the one. You see, the people in Grasmere want to take care of their own. These children don't need social workers and psychologists—just a roof, warm clothes, and a lot of love. I wrote a proposal covering each of those aspects which you should've received by now."

"I received it. And filed it."

In the circular file, more than likely. "Then you see we have the children's welfare foremost in our plans."

"Miss Markum, you must understand that in order to maintain our status we must adhere to certain standards. Unfortunately, your project comes nowhere close to what I can allow."

Rita's heart sank. She'd given several thousand dollars to the project herself, but it wasn't nearly enough. Even after they built the house, the budget had to include operation and maintenance costs, and more importantly, the children needed money for care. If ever there was a time to cowboy up, it was now. By hook or by crook, those children would be cared for right here in Grasmere where they belonged.

She spent the rest of the day making applesauce—three dozen pints of it. Rita didn't care if she ever ate another bite of the stuff. Her mom hovered, always wanting to help and not the least bit comfortable with having someone else take over her kitchen.

"You might as well get used to it." Rita screwed rings on the last seven jars. "You won't be cooking for at least a couple of weeks yet." At least, not if she had anything to say about it.

This was the first time in Rita's memory that her mom had ever shown physical infirmity. She'd cooked meals, collected eggs, and fed cattle through bouts of colds and flu, sprains and pulls, rashes and bruises.

"How many head of cattle do you have now? And who's feeding them?"

"Fifty-three head, and I'm feeding them, of course. They're

my cattle."

"I'll be feeding them as long as I'm here, starting tonight. Just let me know what and where."

"Luke can feed them. You don't need nasty calluses on your pretty hands. Rita, I told you not to come out here. I'd have done fine by myself, and you have a busy schedule to keep—and a rich man on a string, too."

Rita placed the final batch of jars in the canner and turned the burner to high. "I refuse to let you go through this by yourself. You'd never leave me in a lurch if I needed help. Besides, David will do fine for a few weeks, and when I get back I'll work out the final details of the wedding."

While the jars cooled and sealed, Rita took the apple peelings to the backyard and threw them to the chickens. No matter where she looked, memories flooded in. A sawhorse with steer horns nailed to one end leaned against the barn. Her dad had tried to teach her to rope, but she'd never been very good. She tried hard, though, because she didn't want him to show her again, since every time he threw the rope he was in deep pain even though he didn't let on. But she knew. And it was hard for him to keep his balance in the wheelchair.

Enough reminiscing.

Back in the house, she wiped the sticky counters clean. This sort of work was exactly why she'd rather be number-crunching in Seattle. She could buy applesauce at Safeway.

"I guess we'd better get you some supper, Mom. It's nearly five o'clock and you aren't supposed to eat anything after six." She grabbed some green beans and a spaghetti squash from the cupboard.

Judy limped to the refrigerator and opened it. "I'll fry up the chicken."

"No, you won't!" Rita commandeered the chicken and led her mother back to her chair. "I didn't come clear out here from Seattle just to watch you stand in front of a hot stove on your sore knee."

"I'm not too hungry, so don't fix much for me."

"I'll fix a whole meal. Remember, it'll be a long time before you get to eat again." Rita hated to admit it, but she actually enjoyed doing things for her mother. It was kind of a payback, she supposed. Her mother had always knocked herself out trying to meet her daughter's needs, and most of her wants, too. "You're probably just nervous."

"How long are you planning to stay?"

Rita picked up a spatula and scooted the Crisco around in the hot skillet. "The doctor said you won't be up and about for six weeks, so that's how long I'll be here. I had some vacation coming, plus I took four weeks' unpaid leave."

Her mother sighed, then cleared her throat in that way of hers when she had something uncomfortable to ask. "So doesn't your David mind you being away from him?"

Dredging the chicken breasts in seasoned flour, Rita placed them in the pan. Did David mind? Yes. He'd expressed his disappointment that she wouldn't be there to supervise construction of their new home in an upmarket neighborhood on Mercer Island. And he'd insisted that she finish the financial reports she'd been helping him with. Actually, *helping* wasn't quite the correct term, since she'd done all the research, calculations, spreadsheets, and write-ups herself. But he'd do the same for her.

"Rita? You're a million miles away."

"Oh, I'm just concentrating on the cooking. I don't cook much in Seattle, you know."

She glanced at her mother, who wore a decidedly skeptical expression. Darn, she never could fool her mother. Yes, coming here was a pain in the rear, but her mother needed her, and she was here. That was that.

"Brody's as handsome as ever, isn't he?"

Warmth crept up Rita's cheeks as she concentrated on stringing the beans. "Yes, Mom. Handsome as the devil." Her knife slipped and she nearly took a hunk of her thumb along with the string. For the first five years after she'd left home,

Brody had been her first hope when she woke up and her last dream before she drifted off to sleep. But she was over him now.

"A helpful neighbor, too."

"I'm sure he is."

"He and Luke came over this spring and plowed and harrowed my garden."

"That's nice." She rinsed the beans, plopped them in a saucepan with water and salt, and put them on the stove to boil.

"When we had a fundraiser for the children's home, Brody donated two beeves."

"Two's more than one."

"Yup. And when the bills closed in on me, he lent me some money. I told him I'd go over and fix him a meal and clean his house once a week."

"I bet he needed his house cleaned more than he needed the money."

"Rita! Well," her mother conceded, "there's some truth to that. Anyway the agreement goes through January."

Rita froze. It was September. Did her mother expect her to clean Brody's house and fix his meals? Obviously, yes. She squeezed her eyes shut and sighed. Of course she would help her mother meet her obligations, but going to Brody's house every day seemed a bit above and beyond the call of duty.

"There's one thing, though. I don't want you spoiling things with your city boyfriend."

"Why would you think I'd do a stupid thing like that? David and I are in love."

Her mother frowned in obvious doubt. "A man like Brody can sweet-talk the chirp right out of a sparrow. Stay away from his charm, or you'll end up barefoot and pregnant, married to a broken-down cowboy. There's no future in that, honey."

Her mom was right. Rita didn't know how she could avoid melting like a teenage virgin every time he glanced her way. But that's exactly how he made her feel.

Five a.m. came way too soon for Rita. Armed with an insulated cup of strong coffee, she felt a little sorry for her mother, who could only have the smallest sips of water, and only for meds, before her surgery.

"I'll warm up the car."

"No need. Brody and Luke will be here in no time."

"Hmph! You've been telling me all my life, 'No cowboys,' yet here you are, letting not one, but two of them take you to the hospital."

On cue, an extended-cab pickup with a camper that had *Brody Alexander—Rodeo Bullfighter and Clown* emblazoned on the side pulled into the driveway, over the grass, and rolled to a stop directly in front of the kitchen door. Luke opened the passenger door and made a gimpy, but hasty jump out. "Ready?"

Before Rita could respond, Judy hobbled out of the house. Luke helped her into the back seat and buckled her in. Rita wasn't sure what she thought of such an intimate gesture, but maybe she made too much of it. Then Luke hopped in beside Judy—amazingly agile for an old busted-up bullrider—and Rita instantly took a disliking to him. He seemed entirely too familiar with her mother.

Rita held her tongue, but later she'd give her mother the same lecture that she'd received when she was a teenager and again last night—*No cowboys!*

Brody waved at Rita and she nodded back, doing her best to remain calm at the sight of him—bullfighters counted as cowboys. No, they were worse than cowboys.

Gripping her travel mug of strong coffee, she climbed into the passenger seat beside him. She had no idea he had a brand new rig, and she wondered why he had chosen to drive the old beater Chevy the day before. But it was none of her concern. *He* was none of her concern. She'd told herself that the entire previous sleepless night.

In fact, she wouldn't even think about him.

Or how his Old Spice after-shave made her want to run her fingertips along his jaw.

Or how he was only a foot away from her and she could easily reach out and put her hand on his thigh.

Or how he somehow pulled her gaze to him without doing a thing.

She squeezed her eyes shut. This two-hour drive promised to be a very long one. For sure.

Brody stole a glance at the pretty filly sitting in the passenger seat every chance he got. He just couldn't get enough of her, even though her stiff posture and pinched lips spelled *stay away*. He should pay heed, too, because he smelled trouble lurking about her tempting flowery perfume.

But then, he never could resist a challenge.

Not that he'd had many when it came to women. Challenges, that is. He'd always had all the women he wanted. As long as they stayed their distance afterward, he was a happy man. A few times he'd been momentarily caught in some bucklebunny's net, but not often and certainly not recently.

He glanced at her again. *Keep your eyes on the road and drive, buddy.* This was going to be a long trip.

Ninety minutes later, the hospital finally came into view—a sight Brody never thought he'd actually be happy to see—and he pulled into the passenger loading zone of the Outpatient Surgery Center.

A nurse who sat on the bench sipping a Diet Coke broke into a wide grin when she saw him and waved. He rolled down the window.

"Hey, Brenda."

She ran to his door. "Hi, Brody! You here for another patch job?"

"No, darlin', I brought the neighbor lady in for knee surgery. Do you have Judy Markum on your list?"

"Sure do. I'll get an orderly out here to wheel her in." As she turned to go back into the building, she asked, "Want to go out for drinks later?"

He shook his head. "Next time. I'm taking Mrs. Markum home after surgery. Two-hour drive, you know."

The nurse shrugged. "Darn. But I'll see you around today."

After she left, Brody killed the motor and got out of the rig to open Rita's door. He knew he was in a heap of trouble the second he saw the blaze ignite in her eyes. Women were a puzzlement.

"I knew I should've brought Mom here myself!" She jumped out and jammed her hands on her hips. "Do you know the odds are that you'll be in the hospital three times this season?" She leaned forward. "And did you know that by the time you reach thirty-five, that number will probably increase by two?"

Stepping closer, she wagged her finger in his face. "And did you know that odds are that if you've dated that nurse, that you've probably dated—*if* you call it that—at least six nurses at this hospital alone? That is, of course, if there are twenty single women working here." She swatted her hands together, turned her back on him, and stomped off.

Brody realized his jaw sagged at her ridiculous calculations, and snapped his mouth shut. She was wrong. He'd only dated four women from this hospital. He'd spent considerably more time in the Boise hospital.

Luke stepped up, shook his head, and hooked his thumbs over his belt buckle. "What did ya say to crinkle her hair, Romeo?"

"Beats me." Brody rubbed the stubble on his chin as he watched an orderly wheel a chair toward the pickup. "But that woman needs to do a little more livin' and a lot less math."

Chapter 2

Well, it's seven a.m. and Guinevere should be executing phase two of our plan right about now. She was a little reluctant about the whole thing, worried about getting her fur ruffled as all skunks are, but she finally agreed to help after Perseus said he would as well.

I wanted to sneak into the camper, too, but my ears brush the cabinets and that annoys me. My ears are perfectly shaped and my hair lies just so. I don't like it rumpled. At any rate, I didn't see a way to get into the camper without Brody noticing, and he always checks the corral and barn to make sure I'm there before he goes anywhere.

But back to the plan. I remember way back before Rita went to college, she batted her eyelashes and wiggled her hiney every time she saw Brody. And Brody always looked, and I mean always. No, not like he looks at the bucklebunnies—it was different with her. And yesterday I saw that it's different now. He tries a little bit harder, but his easy charm still gets all choked up. He's a goner.

Yup, whether either one of them know it or not, they belong together. Yesterday was only the beginning. I have lots more tricks up my saddle blanket, and by this time next year we ought to have a little Brody to take care of.

Brody watched Rita walk alongside the wheelchair as the orderly wheeled her mother to the surgery center. In fact, he watched them go all the way up the sidewalk—partly to make sure of his own safety from the unpredictable woman, and partly because her buns had such a sweet wiggle.

After they'd entered the building, he turned and opened the camper door. Luke leaned against the pickup, making no effort to contain Perseus, who bounded onto the pavement. The poor dog was full of pent up energy.

"Stay, Perseus." Brody shut the door. "I'd better get some water for him. He's been cooped up for two hours."

"Yup." Luke nodded. "He could use a pee, a drink, and a run. Why don't I take him out and you head in with the ladies?"

"Coward." Perseus leapt four feet in the air and laid a slimy doggy kiss on Brody's cheek.

"That, and old bones. I need a walk myself. Maybe a pee and a drink, too." Luke grabbed a jug of water from the cab and took off for the field across the street. "C'mon, Perseus. I see tall grass and a ditch full of water. Sounds like a good time to me."

After Luke and the rambunctious dog left, Brody stared at the hospital door, willing himself to join Rita and Judy in the waiting room. He knew right where it was.

Damn, he hated hospitals. For bullfighters, hospitals meant lost work and long lectures from orthopedic surgeons. And they meant he'd made a mistake in judgment. One misstep in front of a charging bull and a man ended up in the damn hospital. Again.

It was part of the job, so he had no complaints. As the saying goes, "It's not *if* you'll get hurt, it's when and how bad." But no thrill on earth compared to facing off with an angry bull.

Clowning and bullfighting had been his obsession ever since he could remember. There was no greater rush. Not that his mother understood that. He'd almost rather be stuck in the hospital than in his family's corporate offices—but no one in Grasmere, or the rodeo circuit, for that matter, needed to know anything about his former life.

He took one look at the outpatient doorway and decided he

needed to go for a walk a whole lot more than he needed to sit in the waiting room with a bunch of worried relatives. Besides, he needed the exercise.

After Rita helped her mom fill out the hospital admission papers, insurance forms, consent forms, privacy forms, and forms to say they'd filled out all the other forms, the orderly wheeled Judy into the surgery waiting room. "The nurse will be right with you, Mrs. Markum," he promised as he left the way they'd come.

"Well, it's nearly time."

"You nervous?"

"Not a bit." Rita stared at her, not believing a word. "Okay, a bit. But remember, I'll be asleep the whole time. It's your job to worry." Her mom smiled, just as she did when she told Rita that her dad had gone to Heaven. It wasn't reassuring at all.

At least a dozen patients of all ages filled boxy chairs lining the periphery of the surgery waiting room. Rita wondered what ailments they each had, then dashed the thought from her mind for even considering invading another's privacy. Still, they all seemed as uneasy as she felt—and she wasn't even having surgery.

Her mom tapped her fingers on the chair arm, then clasped her hands over her bosom as if in prayer. Maybe she was. Maybe Rita should join her.

Rita searched for something to divert her attention and focused on the coffee table in the middle of the room. She studied the tall vase of plastic irises perched precariously on a pile of well-worn periodicals in an attempt to avoid looking at anyone. Nevertheless, she caught herself people-watching again.

A young woman sat in the chair opposite Rita and Judy, gazing fondly at her toddler son who stood between her knees, rubbing his lollipop all over her pants. Rita couldn't understand why the woman didn't take the sucker away from the child to prevent more smears on her slacks. But the young mother seemed content to watch her son take a lick, then smear the wet candy on her clothes.

Judy stopped picking her nails and smiled at the boy. "I swear, I didn't have a clean piece of clothing for longer than five minutes until the day I put you on the bus to first grade."

Rita, still befuddled by a mother allowing this behavior, shook her head. "Why on earth didn't you make me stop?"

"Oh, it's a mother thing." Her mom chuckled. "I didn't mind the suckers and the peanut butter so much. It was your boogers on my jeans that got to me."

Rita deemed it best to let the conversation drop, disgusting as it was, although at least it did keep her mother from fidgeting. She'd never known her mother to fidget, even in the most dire of circumstances.

She patted her mom's shoulder. "I'll be right here waiting for you. Everything's going to be all right."

Judy smiled wanly, looking extremely uncomfortable sitting in the wheelchair, and Rita knew that her mom had to be nervous. She'd only been in the hospital once as a patient and that was to have a baby, Rita, twenty-eight years ago. Her mother drummed her fingers on the arm of the waiting room chair.

An old man snorted, then his head drooped to his chest and he started snoring. His wife turned the page of her book and didn't seem to notice.

Rita picked up a dog-eared three-year-old issue of *People Magazine* for want of anything else to do, but before she got past the table of contents, a nurse carrying a clipboard loaded with a raft of papers stepped in front of them. "Are you Mrs. Markum?"

Judy nodded.

"We're ready for you now." She glanced at Rita, then back to Judy. "Is this your daughter?"

"Yes."

The nurse turned Judy's wheelchair toward a hallway in the

rear of the waiting room. "Your daughter may come in with you to help you undress. During the procedure she'll be in a waiting room outside of recovery, where we can keep her informed of your progress. We estimate surgery time to be about an hour. As soon as you show signs of waking up, we'll bring her in to see you and help you dress. You'll be able to go home as soon as you're stabilized and aware."

Rita swallowed a lump in her throat, realizing that the distant concept of surgery was here and now, and that it was *her mother* going under the knife. For a split second she thought about grabbing her mom and running out of the hospital, but in the back of her mind she heard her dad say, "Cowboy up, girl. You've got to show 'em who's boss."

She gathered her mother's crutches and purse, then stood and faced the nurse. "Thank you. We're ready."

Shrieks sounded from the reception area and all hell broke loose when the doors to the surgery waiting room burst open.

"Call animal control!" screamed a nurse as she vaulted onto a gurney.

Blue-shirted orderlies ran toward the exit, nurses fled toward the waiting room—all crashing into each other, falling down, and picking each other up, then dashing off.

The receptionist jumped on top of her desk, screaming, "HELP!"

A little black and white animal the size of a fluffy cat streaked by as a shouting man in coveralls chased it. He held a blanket at arm's length—presumably for the animal's imminent capture, but probably for his own protection.

The young mother snatched her son from the floor and held him to her breast. "I wanna pet the kitty!" the boy cried.

The critter scurried under the chairs, completely circling the room. Twice. People either jumped on their chairs, or froze, huddled into little balls. Rita dropped one of her mom's crutches and prepared to use the other for a baseball bat when the frenzied animal made a bee-line for her.

"Come over here, you little devil!" the animal's pursuer

cursed, shaking a bed sheet as if the critter would jump into it.

The elderly man boomed, "Huh? Did you say something, Gertrude?"

His wife patted his knee. "No, Harley. Go back to sleep."

"Get that cat!" her mother's nurse yelled, as if shouting would help the man catch it sooner.

Judy sat quietly, smiling as if she knew this would happen all along. "Such a to-do over a scared kitty."

Rita put the other crutch down, ashamed that she'd been close to panicking, too. "Yes, they're just scaring the poor creature more, poor thing."

The custodian chased the animal into a corner, but it performed a speedy U-turn on the wall. After knocking the plastic flowers off the coffee table, it clambered up Rita's jeans, then nestled itself in her arms. The little beast shivered like a paint-shaker.

Only then did she realize she held a skunk!

"Omygawd," she murmured, not wanting to scare it any more. One false move and she'd have no friends for years. Decades, even. She stood stone still and closed her eyes, praying that *someone* would do *something*.

When she finally worked up the nerve to open her eyes, she saw the skunk peering at her inquisitively. The animal had stopped trembling. But that didn't remedy the impending odor problem. She continued to stay put, waiting for a white knight to rescue her. Cursing the danged knight for not being there. *Now.*

"Who's responsible for this?" a stern-looking nurse demanded.

"Shhh," hushed Rita, her mother, and her attending nurse.

The surgery waiting room door slid open with a *whoosh* and a silhouette of a hunky man strode toward them. Rita couldn't help but think it was her knight—tall, broad-shouldered. . .oh, dear, but that strut! It could only be. . .

Brody!

"What's all the commotion?" he asked.

The Stern One held up her hand like a traffic cop and marched over to him. "Do not panic or make noise," she ordered in a low, calm voice, enunciating every syllable. "We have a skunk in the building, and I suggest you wait outside until the problem is rectified."

"Maybe I can help. I have a trained. . ." He slapped his forehead. "Oh, God. Show me this skunk. It could be mine."

The nurse led him to Rita. The skunk hadn't moved a muscle, and neither had she. But one look at Brody's calm in the face of disaster and she was ready to throw the stupid animal at him.

"Yup, that's Guinevere, all right." He reached out to take the skunk, brushing Rita's breast ever so slightly. But not slightly enough that she didn't feel a tingle clear down to her toes.

He grinned at the Stern One. "Don't worry, she's descented."

The nurse huffed up like a cobra. "Mis-ter. . ."

"Alexander, darlin'. Brody Alexander, bullfighter and rodeo clown, at your service." He smiled and, bowing, doffed his Stetson.

Quite chivalrous for a rogue. Rita figured he'd met his match, though. Nurse Iceberg couldn't be melted by his charm.

"Mister Alexander, it is highly unsanitary, not to mention disruptive, for you to allow your wild animals to roam the hospital. Maybe even illegal!"

Brody looked properly contrite, but then that practiced charming smile broke out again. "How about we go show the children a few skunk tricks? I have all the skunk's papers in my rig, so we can do it up good and proper." He held his hat to his chest. "And Starbucks after? Just you and me."

The Stern One turned into Menopausal Simpering Coquette right before Rita's eyes. It was amazing. And downright disgusting.

"Well," the nurse responded, gazing at him like a starry-eyed schoolgirl, "I *am* off shift. I could spend an hour or so with you. For the children, of course."

"Yes, for the children. And coffee after."

"Well. . ."

"I'm buying, pretty lady."

Rita couldn't decide whether to laugh or puke as she watched the two of them get into the elevator—especially when he turned and winked at her. Winked! Rita pretended to fuss over her mother, hoping he didn't see the blush that warmed her face.

He had just demonstrated why no sane woman should ever fall in love with a cowboy. Love 'em and leave 'em. That's what they all did. Whatever it took to get a lady in the sack. Most of them were quite successful—in a charming way, of course. But a middle-aged nurse? He'd gone too far.

"Let's go to the dressing room now," her mom's attending nurse urged. "Your room's ready and the anesthesiologist is early. Your daughter can follow us, and I'll show her to the other waiting room after she helps get you ready for surgery."

Rita, clenching her fists, followed the two ladies. Too bad she'd ever met Brody Alexander. She just hoped that her ridiculous lust for him would go away.

But it hadn't in ten years, and the prognosis didn't look so hot—actually, entirely too hot.

"Hey, there."

Rita looked up to see Mr. Stud grinning like he'd just slain another dragon. He probably could, too, if any dragons were around. And he probably would. At least he was skunkless—and sans the Simpering Coquette.

"You can read a lot of magazines in three hours." Rita flipped the magazine closed. "What do you want to know about Tom Cruise?"

Brody sat in the chair beside her. "Nothing. I don't read that sort of stuff."

"I don't suppose you read much." *Or at all.*

"Nope. Used to, though."

Yeah, right. Probably the Sunday comics and *Western Horseman.* "Oh? What did you read?"

"Uh. . ." He shrugged. "Books."

That's what she thought. It didn't take a lot of intellectual stimulation to woo women or run in front of bulls. But it did take a charming personality for the first, and a well-toned body for the second—both of which he had in spades. And the source of extreme irritation for her.

Her face flushed hot, and she didn't doubt red crept up her cheeks. She only hoped he'd think the cause was something other than this inconvenient attraction—yes, inconvenient was a genteel word for it—that just wouldn't go away.

In fact, she'd thought about kissing him when she should have been worrying about her mother. Rita sighed and waved the magazine in front of her face to ward off the guilt and the heat. A decent daughter wouldn't be thinking about kissing a no-good cowboy while her mother was in surgery. And no decent woman would even consider kissing anyone other than her own fiancé!

The nurse came in. "Your mother's awake and we're dressing her. You can come in, now." She looked at Brody and smiled. "If you're driving, you can bring your vehicle to the side door and we'll meet you in about fifteen minutes."

Brody practically bounced to his feet. Obviously, five minutes of sitting with her was five minutes too long for him. "Yes, ma'am." He grabbed his hat and beat feet out the front door.

Rita stood and followed the nurse, only to find her mother sitting on the side of the bed, giggling. She raised an eyebrow at the male nurse attending.

He chuckled. "You never know how a patient will do with anesthetic. Sometimes they get, well, a little loopy. You should have an interesting trip home."

Judy looked up at him. "You know," she said with a cockeyed smile, "with a nice western shirt and a pair of tight Wranglers, you'd be welcome to park your boots under my bed." She patted him on the butt.

"Mother!" Rita couldn't believe that her mom would even *think* such a thing.

The nurses didn't seem to hear, or at least be bothered, by her mother's outlandish behavior and proceeded to move Judy to the wheelchair. They carefully lifted the bandaged encased knee to ensure it didn't bump against the railings. Rita imagined the hospital must own stock in the gauze and bandage companies based on the huge blob wrapped around her mother's leg.

The male nurse handed her a couple of bottles of pills. "One's an antibiotic. Give her one tablet three times a day. The other bottle is pain medication—two tablets every four hours as needed." He gave her a paper. "This explains the after-care. We've had your mother sign it, but has anyone gone over it with you?"

Rita took the instructions. "Yes, this morning."

"If you have any questions, or if she starts running a fever, call us right away. The number's at the top of the page."

Judy giggled. "I have your number, big boy."

"Let's get out of here," muttered Rita. Maybe the outside air would calm her mom. It sure couldn't make her any worse.

She got worse.

Rita swore her mom's mouth had run like the Kentucky Derby ever since they put her in the danged pickup.

"Why, I'm just so proud of my daughter! She's on her way to being an ashuary."

"Ashuary?" Brody asked.

Rita kept her gaze trained on the road, afraid of what her mother might say next. "Actuary."

"Yup, an ashuary," Judy continued. "My daughter has passed all sorts of tests. She's so smart. I tell her, 'Don't marry no damned cowboy,' but I get a little worried when she's around you. But she's got a fancy city dude convinced to marry her, so she ought to be okay."

"Mother!" Rita wished she could flatten herself and crawl under the seat cover.

"Luke," Judy went on, unfazed, "you get better lookin' every day for an old busted up cowpoke. What you say we have a little ron-day-voo?"

Rita looked back just as Luke started to pat her mother's shoulder. "Don't you touch her, buster."

Luke jerked his hands back. Rita relaxed and faced front, satisfied, at least for the moment.

Brody drove with one hand on the wheel and held the other hand beside his face obscuring his mouth, as if stifling a laugh. Rita's blood boiled. It just showed the coarseness of cowboys— and why she'd never want one. Okay, she'd never want one for keeps. They'd be great if a girl was looking for a boy-toy. Which, of course, she wasn't.

"My daughter can do any math. Anything you can imagine. Boy, I feel funny. Luke, would you feel my cheeks?"

"Which set?"

Rita whirled her head around again. "LUKE!"

"Any set you'd like, big boy," Judy smiled at him and batted her eyelashes. Her *eyelashes*, for Pete's sake! Rita watched her own mother flirt unabashedly. This was getting more revolting by the minute.

"Well, sugar, I think we ought to wait until you're feeling a might better, then we'll see which cheeks you want me to feel." He took off his hat and fanned it in front of Judy's face. "Does this feel good?"

"Mmmmm."

Rita relaxed her shoulders, hoping her mother had said all she was going to.

"You're a fine man, Luke," her mother cooed.

Rita tensed again, knowing whatever Judy said next, it would most certainly be embarrassing. She seriously considered stuffing a sock in her mother's mouth.

"Brody's a fine man, too," Judy went on. "Really fine, in fact. I just hope Rita can keep her hands off him. Why, before she went off to college, I thought Brody would get in her pants for sure. But I guess she fended him off, 'cause near as I know, he never got to her."

Nearly lightheaded, Rita breathed deep to keep her composure. Was it legal to strangle your mother if she were on drugs? Surely it ought to be.

Worse, both she and Brody knew Rita had been the aggressor. She glanced at him. He stared at the road, obviously trying to fake invisibility—but a hint of a smile played on his lips.

Then he winked at her. She wanted to smack that crooked smile right off his taunting, handsome—okay, a little beat up, but handsome nevertheless—face. The jerk.

Resigned that her mom's mouth would continue to motor for the next two hours, Rita changed the subject. "How're the plans for the children's home coming?" Several children needed a permanent home, and Phyllis was willing to keep them if they had a place; otherwise, the state might find out and take the kids some god-awful place, like a city. One thing about country people—they took care of their own.

"Well, when Phyllis gets a little farther along on it, we're going to have Brody and Luke work with the children."

Brody cocked his head and raised an eyebrow. "I'm not home much for six months out of the year. You'd better rethink that."

"Oh, but Luke is. And it'll give me an excuse to come see him."

"Mother!"

Judy giggled, then groaned. "Ooh, that hurt."

Luke scooted closer to her. "Do you need a pain pill? I have a jug of water right here."

"Yes, another pain pill would be good," Rita agreed.

"Maybe she'll fall asleep."

Brody shook his head. "Too soon. Don't want to OD her— she's not used to taking medication. That's why she's acting half-drunk right now."

"*Half*-drunk," Rita muttered.

"And did you know," Judy went on, ignoring the others' comments, "that Rita is getting funding so we can build a new house? She's even contacted the MOMMI Foundation. It's a charitable organization she found out about through her work."

Brody whirled his head to look at Judy, turning the steering wheel as he did so. The pickup nearly swerved off the road, whipping the passengers about, but he expertly regained control. "MOMMI?"

Rita looked back at her mother. "Are you okay?"

Judy grinned crookedly back at Rita. "That was fun. Can we do it again?"

"Not. Anyway, the MOMMI Foundation turned us down flat. No state accreditation—no money. Period. So we have to look elsewhere. A bunch of snobs operate that place anyway. The woman I talked to, Caroline, is a Class-A bitch. I'd really rather not have to deal with them." Rita hoped she could keep her mother channeled to the children's home conversation and maybe she'd quit talking about embarrassing things.

Her mom didn't respond, and when Rita looked back, she saw her mother fast asleep with her head on Luke's shoulder.

"You can relax now."

Rita jolted at Brody's voice. Yeah, right. Not while she was in the same latitude and longitude as he was. But at least her mom had quit running off at the mouth. For the time being.

Rita prayed that her mother would sleep for the rest of the long drive home.

Brody thought the seventy-three miles home might as well have been a hundred and seventy-three—the first part with Judy's downright screwy remarks and the rest punctuated by awkward silence. Thank goodness they were almost to

Grasmere.

He'd felt a little sorry for Rita. Her mom's comments had obviously upset her. Still, he'd learned a lot—that Judy felt a lot more than just friendly with Luke, for one. He hadn't been aware of that, and neither had Luke, that he knew of.

Rita wasn't as immune to him as she wanted him to think, for another. Still, her engagement to the city dude prevented Brody from using his charm on her. He had no intention of seducing an attached woman. She was too dangerous for him, anyway. He could smell a woman like her clear in the next state—she wanted a long-term commitment. He wanted a good time.

But her inquiry to the MOMMI Foundation unsettled him. If she stuck her oar in too far, she'd find out a lot more than he wanted anyone out here to know. Maybe he better call his sister and tell her to let loose with the money; otherwise, Rita was likely to poke her nose where he didn't want it.

Luke groaned as Brody pulled onto the Markum's bumpy ranch road and checked the mailboxes.

As he handed the mail to Rita, Brody looked in his rearview mirror and saw that Judy still slept on his shoulder. "Your arm getting a little numb?"

"Nope. Went past that stage more'n an hour ago."

"She looks real content, though. We'll have to wake her to get her in the house."

"Might be easier said than done."

"I can take care of my own mother." Rita didn't sound any too happy.

What an odd one. Most women would be glad to have a couple of men around to haul a sick person in the house. Not Rita—more stubborn than any mule ever born—even Socrates. Brody shook his head. "Darlin', I have no doubt about that, but we'll help her into the house. Help her to bed, if you want."

"I don't want."

"Rita," Judy groaned, "I'm hurting. Let the men help me to

my room."

Rita nodded almost imperceptibly. Brody figured her concessions didn't come often, but even she would bow to her suffering mother's wishes. And he knew the pain that followed knee surgery all too well.

He braked the pickup to a crawl before they got to the washboardy driveway. Slow as he went, the bumps still jostled them this way and that, with an occasional moan from Judy. His heart went out to her, but he couldn't do a damned thing about it. The mile-long lane seemed like a hundred.

He pulled into Judy's yard, still another couple hundred yards of bumps to negotiate. A red Miata with the top down was parked by Rita's Volvo. Who the hell could *this* be? Not only did Judy have company—a city slicker for sure—but Socrates stood in the seat of the car with his front hooves propped on the door. His back hooves were probably poking holes in the passenger seat. Whoever owned that car wouldn't be too happy when they saw him.

Brody rolled down his window as he slowed the pickup. "Get out of that car, you mangy mule!"

"David," Rita whispered, and covered her face with her hands.

Chapter 3

I do not have mange, and I resent his insinuation. Nevertheless, I can hardly wait to hear how our plan worked out from Guinevere and Perseus. That is, if I can get Perseus to hold still long enough and Guinevere to stop trembling from fear. Skunks have no fortitude whatsoever. We mules are often accused of being cowards—or stubborn—but we're most certainly not. We're smart.

For instance, why would a human jump out of a perfectly good airplane? A mule would never do such a stupid thing. Or, in the case of my own human, Brody, why would he taunt an already-mad bull that outweighs him ten times? More befuddling, why would he do it with a broken arm and a concussion?

A mule knows when to leave well enough alone. We're sensible.

But the most incredibly ridiculous thing humans do is to deny their destinies. We all know that Brody has a thing for Rita, and she has a thing for him. So where are the little Brodys?

Humans are just plain slow on the uptake sometimes. All we mules can do is practice the latest of training procedures: set up the situation, wait for the human to make the correct decision, then reward them for even the smallest progress.

Believe me, as dense as humans are, we need a lot of patience to train them. But it can be done.

Still, there are some humans that just aren't worth fooling

41

with. Like the dude that drove to the Markum place in a silly sports car with zippo ground clearance—far less than the little filly's. No one with any brains at all would drive a car like that on backcountry roads. But he looked like a man on a mission, and I'm afraid the mission's name might be 'Rita.'
It's time to rally the forces. This guy has got to go.

As the pickup crept over the bumpy driveway toward the ranch house, Rita's heart pounded. She concentrated on calming herself while she cooked up a plan to get rid of David. Fast. Heck, maybe a few mule hooves poking holes in the leather would actually help. At any rate, she didn't want him to know what a country bumpkin she had been—although it was a little late now.

Brody braked the pickup slowly, but not gradually enough for Rita. Nothing good could come from David's visit and she was embarrassed for him to see her humble beginnings. The mule hopped out of the sports car and trotted to his owner's door, walking alongside the slow-moving rig. Rita rustled her papers and gathered her things, hoping she'd look too busy to carry on a conversation.

Brody reached out the pickup window and patted the mule's nose. "Luke, you gather up Judy's stuff while I start the generator. Rita, you go in the house and get her bed turned down."

As if she wanted to go in that house. "I'll get Mom ready."

"No, she'll need to lie down." Brody steered the pickup toward the walkway. "Besides, you need to let your boyfriend know you're here. Unless you want me to."

Not in a dozen blue moons. "I'll go."

She looked out her window and gasped. David scowled as he walked toward the pickup. He opened the door and she jumped out. The only thing worse than him seeing the place where she'd grown up was him seeing Brody and getting the wrong idea about the situation.

A tic in David's cheek and his tousled eighty-dollar haircut gave away his frustration. "Do you realize that not one damned light works in this house? Besides, I couldn't find anywhere to recharge my laptop."

His laptop? She was practically speechless. He could at least act as if he were concerned about her mother—or even jealous of Brody—but never did she think he'd be more worried about his computer.

Brody had gone to the back of the house and within moments she heard the generator's shrieking starter struggle to get the old thing to kick in. None too soon, it settled down to a low rumble.

"What's that noise?" David asked.

She pivoted and grabbed her things out of the pickup, clenching her teeth. "In case you're wondering, my mom is fine."

"Oh, yes. I came to see how she was doing."

Luke came around the pickup, handed the crutches to Rita, and opened Judy's door. "Let me hold you around the waist, sugar, and I'll lift you right up and stand you on the ground. Remember not to put any weight on that bum knee."

"I won't." Her mom sounded shaky, but game.

"Brody and I will help you in."

Beauty trotted to the pickup and barked once, a slobber dripping from her dewlap.

"That's the God-awfulest, ugliest dog I ever saw!" David remarked. "Is this a Lassie experiment gone wrong?"

He belonged in the city—as did Rita—but he didn't have to say mean things about the dog. She scowled at him. "Her name's Beauty. She's half bloodhound and half collie, and, for your information, is a very loyal and well-behaved dog."

And, Rita conceded, not all that beautiful. Beauty had the loose skin, dewlap, and heavy body of a bloodhound, but the bark, heavily frilled collar, and long, skinny head of a collie.

David nodded. "That was a joke."

"Not funny. I'll go turn the bed down." Rita dashed into the house, hoping David wouldn't follow. He did. She thought about throwing the crutches on the ground to trip him. David simply couldn't stay. It was bad enough that he knew she grew up in a podunk place that didn't even have electrical service, but who knew what Brody might tell him.

She flipped on the light in her mother's room and quickly turned down the bed. David stood in the doorway. "I didn't try the lights in here. Why do these lights work and the rest of the lights don't?"

Rita sighed. "They all work now. Brody just turned on the generator. Don't you hear it?"

"Who's this Brody?"

She whacked the pillow to fluff it. Then punched it again because it felt good. "My mother's neighbor," she said, hoping she sounded nonchalant. "He owns the ranch you passed through to get here. Luke's his ranch manager. Now get out of the doorway so they can put Mom in her bed."

David stepped aside, letting the men and Judy pass by him. "I need you to take a look at the report and make a few changes."

"Not now!" She gritted her teeth 'til her jaw ached, waiting for him to have the decency to leave the room. He didn't.

"Move." She placed her hand on his chest and pushed him backward to the bedroom door. "Go sit in the living room. Or the kitchen. Or in Seattle. We have work to do here."

"Are you trying to get rid of me?"

Yes! "I have to prepare her supper, David. Go entertain yourself. Recharge your computer. Whatever."

Ignoring him, she gently placed some pillows under and around her mom's newly-repaired knee and pulled the bedcovers over her. Luke put a glass of water on the nearby nightstand.

"Hey, buddy," Brody warned, "the lady just had surgery. Let her rest."

Rita flinched at Brody's tone. She'd been so consumed with getting rid of David that she forgot about the two other men she didn't want there, either.

"I left the report on the kitchen table," David said as he retrieved his laptop and disappeared into the living room.

Luke patted the back of her mother's hand. "Let us know if you need anything."

Judy nodded.

A man's strangled yelp echoed through the house. "RITA!" It was David.

She, Brody, and Luke elbowed each other trying to be the first in the living room. As they burst through the doorway, they froze when they saw her fiancé standing on the couch with Socrates nipping playfully at his kneecaps.

"Get this wretched beast away from me!"

Luke chuckled, shook his head, and went into the kitchen.

Rita, inclined to do the same thing, stomped over to Socrates and grabbed his halter. "Good gravy, David, get your dirty shoes off my mother's couch. And if you can't even fend off a dinky little mule, you have a serious problem."

She led the mule to Brody, who leaned casually against the doorframe. "Can't you control your animals? Take your stupid mule and go home. Take your dog and skunk, too. And Luke."

"Rita," her mother called with a shaky voice.

Grateful for an excuse to separate herself from David and the smirk on Brody's face, Rita hurried to tend to her mom.

David stepped off the couch, calling after her, "So when can we go over the report? I need some changes."

She left the room, blowing her bangs off her forehead. Who said corporate life was stressful? They sure as heck hadn't been in Grasmere for a day.

Back in the bedroom, she found her mother struggling to sit up in bed. "Mom! You're supposed to be resting."

"Honey, nature calls. You've got to get me to the governor's conference room, no matter what sort of zoo is in the living room." She eased her way to the edge of the bed. Closing her eyes and breathing deeply, she held her bad leg while she shifted it over the side of the bed. Pain clearly got the best of her and she moaned, but pushing herself up with her arms, she tried to stand on her good leg before Rita rushed over to help her. "That mule didn't mess up my carpet, did he?"

"No, Mom." She'd have to clean the dirt off the couch, but she didn't want to trouble her mother with that right now.

"You'd better take care of whatever David wants. You can't keep a man waiting if you expect to get him to the altar."

"I will." She needed to apologize for being so short with him, too, since she'd over-reacted when so many things happened at once, and David's visit was completely un-expected.

"And, honey, invite Luke and Brody for supper. It's downright un-neighborly not to after all the help they've been today."

"But Mom. . ."

"Besides, it's Monday. I always fix supper for them on Mondays. It's part of the agreement."

Rita sighed as she retrieved the crutches, fitted them so her mom had a good grasp on them, and helped her mother into the bathroom. Her mother moaned with each 'hop.' This was going to be a night. She had hoped to get rid of as many men as possible, but it looked like she'd end up with them all for the entire evening.

Brody hadn't wanted to trouble Rita for supper, but he did want to get a better look at this David fellow. Besides, Luke wanted to stay with Judy without seeming too obvious about it.

The evening sun shining on Rita's golden hair had absolutely nothing to do with his desire to hang around. His fingers twitched.

"I'll take the animals home and be back," he told Rita. "Perseus and Guinivere have been cooped up in the camper for two hours, and Socrates. . .well, I don't know what's gotten into the old boy lately. He normally stays put."

"I suppose you'll have to get the stock trailer for him."

"Naw." He patted the mule on the rump. "Socrates, go on home now."

Socrates spared him a glance, tossed his head, then took off at a trot toward Brody's place.

"How do you know he won't wander off someplace?"

Brody smiled, wondering if she really cared about his mule. "He knows where the groceries are."

Luke stepped off the patio. "I'll take the animals on home. You shouldn't be buckin' bales with that busted arm of yours, and the bulls need fed. Won't take me but a half an hour or so." Without waiting for Brody to agree, he climbed into the pickup and headed out.

Rita crossed her arms and raised an eyebrow. "I thought you owned the ranch."

Brody laughed and patted her back. "I do, but Luke's the boss. If you don't believe me, ask him." He lifted his hand and brushed it against her hair, hoping she wouldn't notice. But he just had to know if her hair felt as silky as it looked.

It was silkier. He wanted to draw her to him, taste those full, rosy lips and drink in her warmth. Even as he brought his hand back to his side, the memory of her softness lingered on his fingers. He ached to touch a whole lot more than her hair.

"I, uh, have to get supper on." She made a dash for the house.

He cursed himself for being so affected by an attached woman, and followed her, trying not to notice how her golden hair brushed her neck. Damn. He should have taken the animals home himself. He followed her flowery scent into the house, but slowed as he approached the door.

She had already started to haul food out of the refrigerator by the time he moseyed into the kitchen. David sat at the table, staring at his laptop screen. Brody couldn't imagine a man paying more attention to a computer than a beautiful woman.

"Here." She handed him a dishpan of potatoes, a pot, and a knife. "You have KP."

He held up his broken arm, displaying his cast. "Might get my cast wet."

"Deal with it, cowboy. If you can dash in front of bucking bulls, you can peel spuds." She took an onion from the drawer beside the sink. "David, put away that computer and chop these onions."

"I don't do onions," he muttered without looking away from the screen.

She slammed the laptop shut, and plopped a paper plate, onions, and a knife in front of him. "You do today."

He grimaced, then gathered his papers and laid them on the laptop safely away from the pungent vegetables.

Two points for Rita, Brody started to say, but decided it best to shut up and peel. Loverboy would do well to follow suit. Rita seemed a bit surly—and dangerous.

She slapped some hamburger in a cast-iron skillet, turned the burner on high, and chopped the livin' daylights out of it. Brody couldn't contain a quiet chuckle. He hoped it was loverboy's neck she was hacking—not his.

Brody rinsed the pot of peeled potatoes and ran clean water into the pot. "Where's the salt?"

She grabbed the saltshaker from beside the stove and slammed it on the counter beside him. "Set the table after you get those spuds on to cook."

David smirked, but Brody was plenty willing to do a little kitchen duty to spend more time with Rita—and to figure what on God's green earth she saw in David.

"Keep chopping, tiger," she snapped at her boyfriend.

Looking like a kid caught playing hooky, her boyfriend resumed his duties, while Rita slung hash like a pro. Brody would've bet that David was a virgin onion-chopper.

"I didn't know you could cook," David said. Then one eyelid started to flutter, and he wiped it with his hand—the one that held the onion. Tears streamed down his face.

Brody worked so hard not to laugh that his cheeks hurt. Served the jerk right. "Sad job, huh?" He wetted a paper towel and handed it to teary city slicker, who jammed it on his eye and moaned.

Rita grabbed the chopped onion and threw it in the pot, showing her fiancé no sympathy at all.

"Hey," Brody said as he whacked David's shoulder in a good-ol'-boy punch, "maybe you could work this to your advantage, and get Rita to work on your report for you."

David smiled slightly and sent Brody a super-secret-spy nod. "Honey, are you about ready to help me with the report? I have to leave early in the morning to catch a dinner meeting tomorrow night. And I need the report at the meeting."

"Who's the meeting with?" Rita asked, obviously in better humor since supper was well on its way to completion. She washed her hands, dried them, and sat at the table beside David. "The pope?"

Okay, maybe not so good of humor.

"I don't know their names, but apparently I can't get promoted to vice president until I speak with the owners of Pettybottham Enterprises."

Brody's jaw tightened.

"They're the ones who requested the report in the first place," David continued. "I won't be meeting with the CEO, though. Apparently, he's sending his mother, if you can imagine that. Of course, if my name were Broderick Pettybottham the Fourth, I wouldn't show my face, either."

Brody gritted his teeth and counted backwards from ten.

"He showed his face and more in *Ladies' World Magazine.*"

Brody stifled a groan.

Rita laughed and patted David's hand. "We'd better get with the program. I'll look at the modifications I need to make as soon as we're done with supper."

"Rita?" All three of them looked toward Judy's bedroom.

Rita hurried in, calling to Brody, "Set the table. Dinner's almost ready."

Still seething, he gathered the mail and picked up David's

laptop and the report. Waterson Enterprises—one of his family's holdings, for sure. He wondered if his mother knew what sort of dipshit she would be interviewing.

"So why's Rita writing your report for you? Is she your secretary?"

David laughed—practically a guffaw. "Better not let her hear you say that. You'd be a dead man before you knew what hit you. We work in the same department—Risk Management. She just happens to be a whiz at math, and I need this promotion to pay for our new house, so she's doing most of the report."

"*All* of the report," Rita corrected as she walked back into the kitchen. "We'll have a whopping mortgage on that house we're going to build on Mercer Island."

"Mercer Island, huh?"

"On Lake Washington, east of Seattle."

"Been there," Brody said, wondering which she really wanted—loverboy, or the house. "Pretty snazzy."

Rita smiled at her fiancé, but it seemed plastic. "We like it." She cast Brody a sassy grin and sashayed to the counter.

God, she was sexy. And she deserved more than a house on some stupid lake.

An hour later, Judy, who had insisted on eating at the table, asked Luke to help her back to bed. Brody saw the old foreman wince when he stood, so he motioned for Luke to sit.

"It's hell when you can't even help your own woman to bed," Luke complained.

Rita gasped and Luke held up his hand. "Not to worry, little lady, I misspoke out of frustration."

To help Luke out, Brody took over. "Let's get Judy in her room, Rita."

If Judy's giggles were any indication, the pain medication had kicked in. He braced himself, ready for her to start running her mouth again, and hoped to hell he didn't do that when he took painkillers. He helped her stand.

"You know why I want you to help me to bed?" she asked

after he placed the crutches under her arms.

"No."

"Because he's blond." She pointed at David and giggled again. "Your hair's almost black, and you're handsome as sin, just like Luke." Another giggle. "Too bad you're twenty years too young—I'd give you the ride of your life."

He nearly choked, but hoped Luke hadn't heard that. Although he'd never said anything, a person would have to be in a coma not to notice that Luke was sweet on Judy.

"Mother!"

Brody glanced back at Rita, red-faced and ready to pounce. He felt sorry for Judy, too. She'd be appalled if she ever remembered what she said. "Let's go, Judy."

"And that city boy doesn't have any muscles, either. I bet he wouldn't last fifteen minutes in the sack."

Brody stifled a chuckle. While a bit embarrassing, he had to admit her chatter hadn't hurt his ego one bit. He sure wouldn't want to be in David's shoes, though.

"Oh, crap." Rita looked at David apologetically. "She doesn't do drugs well. Don't pay any attention to her."

"But I want my daughter to marry a rich city boy so she can have all the things a country boy could never give her." More giggles. "Except a good roll in the hay, of course. Cowboys are a helluva lot better at that."

"C'mon, Judy." Brody picked her up, crutches and all, and headed for the bedroom.

She giggled some more. "See what I mean? That wienie in there could never sweep a woman off her feet."

Rita followed them into the bedroom, intending to see to her mother's comfort while getting rid of Brody as fast as possible. His presence only magnified the possibility that David would realize her mother's opinion actually mirrored her own.

Still, David was a nice guy and she felt quite content with him. They had a lot in common and shared the same hopes and dreams. Okay, she admitted, the only thing they had in common were the same hopes and dreams. Most couples based their relationship on lust, and Rita had sworn to have a much stronger alliance than a mere sexual one.

"Brody, you'd better go home." Battle-weary, she ran her fingers through her hair. "I think Mom has done enough damage for one night."

He winked at her as he settled his Stetson just right. Rita wanted to smack him, but there had been little enough civility as it was.

"See you tomorrow, ma'am."

"Bye-bye, Brody." Judy waved. "Bye-bye, Birdie."

He did a mock salute as he left. Rita relaxed, despite the void he left in the room. But she refused to think about the how or why of it.

"Okay, Mom, let's get you tucked in." Gently raising her mother's knee, Rita fluffed the pillow, bolstered other pillows around it should she turn over in her sleep, then tidied up the bedside tray and refilled the water glass.

"Is there anything else you need?"

Her mom's eyelids fluttered as if she were fighting sleep, so Rita walked out of the room. Just as she started to pull the door shut, her mom called her. She went back to her mother's bedside. "Yes, Mom?"

"You have to go over to Brody's tomorrow."

"No, Mom. I need to stay here and take care of you."

"I can't ignore my obligations and expect to rest. Tomorrow is housecleaning day. And there's the fitting, too."

"Fitting?"

"Uh huh. I'm sewing Brody's clown costumes for him now. I can't hardly get down on my knees to do his fitting, and I promised I'd have his break-away jeans done before he leaves Thursday."

Jeans? Oh, no. She wasn't about to put her hands where she'd have to put them to do a fitting. The low ache deep in her abdomen at even the thought convinced her that this was not the job for her. "I'm sure he won't hold you to it."

"That's not the point. If I make a promise, I keep it." Her mother rubbed her eyes, then fell asleep.

Rita hoped her mom would forget all about the fitting when she woke the next day, but doubted it. When she returned to the kitchen, she was relieved to see Brody headed out the door and David pecking away at his laptop at the kitchen table. Lord only knew what they'd been discussing, but David had probably learned way too much about her already. To make sure Brody got good and gone, she followed him outside.

"Don't pay attention to my mother," Rita advised him.

He opened the pickup door and grinned at her. She wished he wouldn't do that—he knew very well what his smile did to most women. Not her, of course, but most women. "It's never hard on a man's ego when a woman thinks he'd be good in the sack."

Rita rolled her eyes. "Well, it was the drugs talking, not her."

"You think so?" Instead of getting in the rig, he strode toward her and put his hands on her waist.

She gazed into his eyes, darker in the evening light. "I know so. I've never heard her say such things." She knew she should pull out of his grasp, but somehow her body didn't obey her mind.

"Doesn't mean she wasn't telling her real thoughts." His face drew nearer hers.

"Don't believe what she said about how I feel about you." Her voice breathless, she knew she should escape, but somehow she couldn't.

"No?" His hands tightened on her waist and his eyes darkened.

She held still, hoping he wouldn't kiss her, but not able to resist staring at his lips. "Lord, help me."

He drew even nearer until their lips met. Against her better judgment, Rita pressed her body into his, craving the strength he offered her, knowing he was forbidden fruit.

He deepened the kiss, touching her tongue with his. Warm tingles skittered through her abdomen and her knees went weak. She sagged against him and he strengthened his hold on her.

"Rita!" she heard David call from the house.

She sprang back and wiped her lips with the back of her hand. "Coming!" Her legs wobbled like jelly and her heart raced.

Brody climbed into his rig, started the engine, then winked at her. "See you, darlin'."

Rita watched him drive off. Breathing deeply, she tried to pull herself together and get her brain in gear. She had committed herself to David and she had no business playing hanky-panky with the local boy-toy. It certainly wouldn't happen again.

But David had *never* kissed her like that.

Brody dialed his mother's number, but hung up before he connected and paced the patio a few more times. If he called her, he knew very well that she'd wheedle him about taking his rightful position as CEO. Damn! She refused to accept that not all people are cut out for corporate life.

Actually, the business didn't put him off so much—what got to him was sitting in the office for the rest of his days. And the back-stabbing cocktail parties where a bunch of people stood around holding mixed drinks sporting the latest cutesy name, pretending they had something to talk about. Meantime, they kept score of who shopped where, bought what car, and belonged to which country club.

He loved his ranch in Owyhee County, and he loved bullfighting and clowning. The people treated him the same as they treated anyone else. But then, they didn't know he could buy half the state without putting a dent in his checkbook. They weren't going to find out, either.

Still, he had to call his mother, lecture or not. He wanted Rita and couldn't have her, but at least he could make sure the person who did the work got the promotion. He owed her that, even if it meant he'd never have his chance with her.

He dialed the phone and she answered on the third ring.

"It's about time you called, Broderick. I wondered when you were going to tell me about your broken arm."

"Fractured, not broken." She made a big deal out of even the smallest incident, which is why he seldom told her about his injuries even though she nearly always managed to find out.

"The healing is the same. Let's see here. . ."

Brody heard her flipping pages—probably of her ever-present notebook where she kept a log of everything and anything.

"I see you haven't broken your left arm yet this year, so at least it's had some time to heal since the last injury."

"Mother, this isn't about me. It's about Pettybottham. Are you meeting with company execs tomorrow?"

"Why Broderick," she chirped, "how did you know about that?"

"Because the man you're meeting with was at my neighbor's house tonight. It's a long story and not of interest to you. What you do need to know is that the man you're considering promoting doesn't do his own work. The report he's submitting to you was written by another Pettybottham employee, Rita Markum."

"Rita Markum—that name's familiar. . ." Brody heard more pages flipping. "Hmmm, she's from Grasmere. One of your former conquests, my dear?"

His jaw tensed. "*No*, Mother."

"I see she has an MBA and is working on her actuary certification."

"I wouldn't know about that, Mother, but she's one smart lady. If anyone deserves the promotion, it's Rita, not her boyfriend."

"Hmmm, boyfriend, eh?"

He knew his mother was scribbling her infernal notes, but

he wished she wouldn't make notes on Rita. "Well, I just thought you might like to know." He changed the subject to one his mother always wanted to talk about. "How's Caroline?"

"Call her yourself. She's your sister, administering your money. Much the same, I would think, as the situation you just mentioned."

He winced. No one was better at cutting a man off at his knees than Mrs. Broderick A. Pettybottham III. And no one was better at cutting a man's heart out than Miss Rita Markum.

"Broderick, are you there?"

"Just make sure Rita Markum gets that promotion."

Chapter 4

Like I said earlier, humans are known to be slow, so we mules have to be very patient.

That phone call to his mother, though, is enough to try my soul. Brody has the hots for that little filly so bad he put up with an interloper just to stay near her a little longer, then he goes and calls his mother, demanding she give Rita a promotion. You gotta wonder.

So I've decided we need a more organized plan to make sure those two balkers have no choice but make the correct decision. I'll have to put more thought into it.

Beauty wants to be in on our plans, too, because she's seen how much her human, Judy, enjoys having Rita around. Beauty says Rita's not half bad, either, and would be a good human for any animal to adopt. Maybe Rita's not as dense as she acts.

But first, I'm going to make sure David leaves like he said he would, and doesn't want to come back any time soon. Then I'll call a meeting with Perseus, Guinevere, and Beauty.

I'll get back to you with our new plan.

Rita could barely keep her eyes open while David leafed through his papers, filed them in his briefcase, and packed the laptop. She'd worked most of the night while David slept on the couch. He'd wanted to stay with her and help, but she insisted he get some rest before the long drive back to Seattle. Besides, she wanted him alert at the dinner meeting with the corporate powers-that-be. Her future depended on David making the most of this rare opportunity.

"I think I've got everything." David kissed her on the cheek. "As usual, you did a wonderful job and I'll make sure they know just who prepared this report."

She smiled, or tried to, considering she'd rather be fast asleep right then. "The main thing is that you were in charge of getting it done, and it did get done. They never intended for you to do it yourself." She glanced around the kitchen. "It's just that the timing was a little inconvenient."

David squeezed her a quick sideways hug. "I'm sorry for being so impatient last night. It's just that I was so worried about this report—it means so much to my career—that I'm afraid I was a bit too insistent. Am I forgiven?"

She wondered if he could ever conjure primal passion like Brody, not that it mattered. Common interests and goals counted in the long term. Passion eventually died.

"You're forgiven, but not if you miss that meeting—as it is, you'll have to average fifty-eight miles per hour, and that includes rest stops. You better get on the road."

"That's my lady!" He saluted and picked up his belongings. "With a slavedriver like you for a wife, I'll never get any rest." He chuckled. "Hopefully, not at night, either."

Entirely too groggy to banter, she hugged him. "Give me a call after the meeting." She walked with him outside and sniffed the sweet scent of sagebrush in the crisp morning air. No place on earth smelled as fresh as Grasmere at dawn. She was surprised to note that she missed it.

"Shoo! Get away!" David shouted.

She didn't pay much attention to him, her sleepy fog dimming his words of distress.

"Rita, do something!"

She turned to see him flailing his arms at Socrates, who rubbed his butt on the front of David's car. Couldn't Brody keep that infernal animal home?

"He's a very small mule, David. Pat his hiney and he'll move."

"He might kick me."

Rita saw Socrates raise his tail. *Oh, dear.* Mule biscuits tumbled onto the Miata's hood.

She shook herself awake, ran over to the mule and led him away. "Socrates, go home." Grabbing a stick, she swept the manure off the hood. 'I'll get some soap and a rag. We need to clean this up before it ruins the paint. Put your stuff in the car, and as soon as I get this wiped up, you can leave."

Five minutes later, she waved, relieved to see her well-planned future drive down the road.

Caroline Pettybottham silently swore at her brother as she hung up the phone. She had reminded Brody that guidelines for funding charities were an important part of staying out of legal hot water. The project he called about, the Grasmere Children's Home, had no state accreditation, no social worker, and no trained personnel. They were fools for even applying for a grant.

Still, he ordered her to approve the application and cut the check. Well, it was his money, so she would. She sighed and opened the Markum file to find the telephone notes she'd taken. Rita Markum, probably another one of Brody's women of dubious character, had been persuasive, but she hadn't a leg to stand on and she'd known it.

The phone rang yet again. Caroline felt like throwing it out the window. She'd only been at work twenty minutes, and this was the fifth darned phone call. Dutifully, she answered.

The phone rang yet again. Caroline felt like throwing it out the window. She'd only been at work twenty minutes, and this was the fifth darned phone call. Dutifully, she answered.

"Caroline, this is your mother."

As if she couldn't distinguish her own mother's voice. "How are you, Mother?" But she didn't need to ask. Caroline knew that her mother had an agenda, and that it would involve her. Again.

"I have it on good authority that Broderick is interested in a lady—a business woman. And she works for our corporation."

"Brody has lots of women, Mother. He can get any woman he wants."

"Not this one."

Caroline sat straighter and switched the phone to her other ear. "You're kidding. Is she married? No," she answered herself, "that couldn't be it. Brody could buy her out of a marriage."

"She's single. Like I said, she works for Pettybottham Enterprises. Brody called me last night after I had retired and told me to promote this woman instead of the young man we're considering."

"Hmmm. Since when has he ever cared who you promoted? And, since when has he even known what was happening with the business at all?"

"Exactly the point," her mother replied. "I want you to go to Grasmere and check her out."

"Grasmere? What's one of our employees doing in Grasmere?"

"She's a neighbor of his. Apparently she's taking care of her mother for a few weeks."

"So what's the woman's name who has my brother so intrigued?"

"Rita Markum. She's our weapon to get Broderick back in corporate headquarters, taking his rightful position as CEO."

Caroline smiled. So that's why he insisted on funding such an absurd project. The neighbor lady must really be something.

"I have a plan, Mother. Talk to you later."

She called her secretary and told her to cut a check for the Grasmere Children's Home, then to arrange travel to Idaho the next Monday.

Rita Markum, she had to see for herself.

Rita heard a car coming and stepped out the door, anxiously awaiting her old friend. Phyllis had called ahead and said she was on her way. Of course, Rita remembered that "on her way" could mean any time from fifteen minutes to two days.

Her gaze followed the trail of dust drawing nearer. "Mom, she's coming!" Phyllis was a few years older than Rita, but the two of them had been fast friends forever. They hadn't seen each other since Rita had visited her mother four Christmases ago.

As the old, multi-primer colored Pontiac turned down their lane, Beauty lifted her head for a look, then rested her snout on her paws again. Rita figured when Beauty saw it was Phyllis, she resumed her nap. No reason to get excited.

But Rita was.

"Do you have the coffee on?" Judy shouted from her bedroom.

"Yes, Mom. And the rolls are cooling."

A few minutes later, the old seventies boat pulled in. Phyllis had a purple bandana tied around her tempestuous red hair, as usual. Rita chuckled to herself, finding comfort in small things that never changed, then hopped off the porch and jogged over to the car, not minding the dust swirling about her.

"Phyllis, I'm so glad to see you!"

The car door let out a croak as Phyllis opened it. She sprang out and engulfed Rita in a massive bear hug. "I missed you so much. You really ought to tell those company honchos to build you an office right here in Grasmere." She gave Rita a kiss on the cheek and another hug.

Arm in arm, they went into the house.

"Mom's in bed where she's supposed to be. She wanted to get up, but I told her you'd beat her with a stick if she was up gimping around when you got here. So you go see her and I'll bring us all some coffee and rolls."

"I'll help with that. I own a diner, you know, and I can carry it all in one shot."

"I do know. You serve people all day, every day. That's exactly why I'm serving you today. So scram! Mom's driving me nuts."

Phyllis left and Rita could hear the two ladies chattering. Her visit would do Judy good. But Rita knew the main reason for Phyllis' visit was to sit with Judy while Rita cleaned Brody's house.

That didn't sit well. She hadn't spent five years in college and four more years of post-graduate study to clean houses. But a promise was a promise, and her mother would drag herself over to Brody's if need be, to live up to her word. That's why Rita had raised no objections to cleaning for him, although she'd rather shoot herself than go in that man's home. Damn!

She placed three cups of coffee and the rolls, butter, and strawberry jam on a tray, then picked it up. Phyllis came running out of the bedroom and nearly upended her, coffee, rolls and all.

"Lord Almighty, I left Tommy in the car!" She dashed out, the screen door slamming behind her. A minute later, she came back in, holding Tommy's hand. "I was so excited, and he's such a quiet boy, I ran off and left him. Shame on me."

As soon as the little boy saw Rita, he yanked his hand away from Phyllis and announced, "I'm four." He splayed his hand in the air, showing four fingers. "I'm gonna be a bullfighter when I grow up, just like Uncle Brody." He sashayed around a kitchen chair swatting it as he went, to show his prowess.

Rita smiled at him. "That was very good. Can you count?"

"Yup." He inched toward the door. "Can Beauty come in?"

"No, she's an outside dog."

Phyllis patted Tommy on the shoulder. "Go on outside and play, but don't go off the grass."

"Yeah, and if I see a snake, I'll wallop it!"

Phyllis cleared her throat and put on a stern expression. "No, you know that if you see a snake, you let Beauty take care of it and you come get me."

"Ah, Mom." He shuffled his foot. "I'm big."

"You heard me." She waved toward the door. "Now, go play." She took the tray from Rita. "You'd better let me carry that. You almost spilled it."

Rita followed her into the bedroom, wanting to point out that Phyllis had nearly run over her, but it seemed like a moot point. Phyllis pretty much did what she wanted.

"Good to see you," Judy said. She reached for the coffee that Phyllis handed her, but pulled her hand back, wincing. "Help me sit up a little straighter, would you?"

Rita sat on the side of the bed while Phyllis went into high gear, seeing no reason to interfere in the redhead's fun. She fluffed and fussed, getting the pillows just so, then propped Judy on them and gave her a cup of coffee. "We'll change the pillowcases before I leave."

"Rita just did that a while ago."

Phyllis' shoulders slumped for a moment, then she perked right back up. "Sent some more bucklebunnies up Triangle Road last Sunday."

Judy laughed. "You didn't."

"I did."

Confused, Rita asked, "Why on earth would you send them to Triangle? It's seventy miles of washboard dirt roads from here."

"That's why." Phyllis had an ornery gleam in her eye. "It's my method of judging their determination factor. "They didn't come back, so I figure they must have found some other cowboy." She shrugged. "Of course, I always write down their license plate numbers in case the sheriff comes out on a Missing Persons report."

"And how often do girls come out?"

"Oh, purt near every weekend. The stupid thing is, Brody's never here on the weekends—in the summer, that is. And the weather's too bad in the winter, so they don't even try." She sat in the chair beside the bed. "Well, very often."

"Hadn't you better check on Tommy?"

"Naw. Beauty's with him. She's the best babysitter you could ask for." She pivoted on the chair and pulled back the curtain to look, despite what she'd just said. Apparently satisfied, she straightened around.

"Do you think Tommy's mother will ever come back?"

"I haven't seen hide nor hair of her for almost three years now. She came for that one visit and said she'd be back in the fall, but she never came. I've had him since he was six months old, you know."

This situation was one that Rita could never imagine happening in Seattle, or any city. A bucklebunny had brought her baby to Phyllis and asked her to take care of him, which is what she'd been doing for three and a half years. Anyplace else, he'd have been a ward of the court. "Do you know who his father is?"

"Heck, his mama don't even know." She picked up the basket of rolls. "Judy, have a roll. Looks like Rita did a bang-up job with them."

"Thanks," Rita said as she took one and broke it apart. "What'll you do if she shows up?"

"Give her a piece of my mind, that's what. Can you imagine letting someone else raise such a precious little boy? Heck, she don't deserve to have him."

"No, but legally, you couldn't keep her from taking him from you."

"Well, I just don't think about it. Anyway, there's a few more kids around here that need homes." She pointed her finger over her shoulder. "Granny Lovell can't take care of the toddler she has because of the rheumatism. Her granddaughter went off to college and left the baby here." She pointed to the right. "Then there's the Abbot boys. Their folks is drunk more often than not. When we get the children's home built, I can keep an eye on all of them."

Rita sighed. "Bad news there. I applied for a grant to every charity I could think of and they all turned us down. Even MOMMI Foundation—they have very few requirements, and even fewer for causes sponsored by employees of Pettybottham Enterprises, and we didn't even meet those. The shrew I talked to ranted for ten minutes about how ludicrous my proposal was, and then hung up on me. I called back two days ago with the same sorry results, so I think we'd better think about organizing another fundraiser."

Phyllis rubbed her forehead. "Well, you tried. We'll think of something." But the quiver in her voice made Rita wish with all her heart she'd had better news. Looking at her watch, Phyllis said, "You better get over to Brody's if you want to get that house cleaned before I have to go. The diner opens at eleven, and it's already nine. I just have to be there a half hour early to get the grills warmed up—I did the prep work last night."

Rita dreaded the task ahead. It brought her way too close to a man who rocked the very lifestyle she'd worked so hard to build.

She nodded at Phyllis and stood. "You ladies have a nice visit. I'll be back soon." After all, how much cleaning could his house need—only one man lived in it and her mom had cleaned it four days before.

Rita stood in the kitchen doorway of Brody's house, utterly astonished. The place looked like it had been rolled over a couple of times and put back on the foundation. Where to start—she had no idea.

The windows still had the same yellow curtains that she'd helped Mamie Johnson put up over ten years ago, just before the Johnsons moved. The once bright curtains hung by dingy threads, and Rita thought the only merciful thing to do was to rip them down and burn them. Oh, well, Brody's curtains were none of her business. The best thing to do was avoid looking at them.

She gathered a bunch of letters from the counter and tossed them on the unopened mail strewn on the table, giving them a quick shuffle to neaten up the pile. His jeans were draped over the kitchen chair—she'd rather not deal with them. Eyeing them cautiously, she chided herself for being such a ninny. She picked them up with her fingertips, not about to touch any more of the fabric than she absolutely had to, and tossed them in the kitchen corner nearest the utility room.

After clearing away a considerable amount of rubble, she tackled the dishes. She had a little more than an hour before she had to get back home, so she stacked the plates in the sink and ran hot, soapy water on them to soak. Only one dirty cast-iron frying pan sat on the stove—Brody and Luke probably fried everything they ate. She turned on the burner and poured hot water into the pan to boil it clean.

Then she quickly gathered the rest of the laundry so she didn't have to think about the testosterone-filled body that had occupied each garment, and shoved it all, colors and whites alike, into a small hamper in the utility room. The worst was yet to come—she dreaded going into Brody's bedroom. She felt like it was a violation of his personal space.

No, it was a violation of hers. She stood in the bedroom doorway, gazing at his unmade bed, unwilling to enter. He might bring out lustful feelings in her, but never in this world would she even consider succumbing to his charms. David filled the bill. David could help her get everything she wanted.

And David didn't undress in the kitchen.

A raspy chirp and scratching at the backdoor reminded her that she didn't have time to waste thinking about the merits of a transient bullfighter. She ducked around the corner to get a look as who or what was there. Guinevere stared back, pleading with her eyes to be let in. She remembered seeing a litter box earlier, so opened the door for the little skunk.

"Come to visit, huh?"

The skunk cocked her head.

Rita laughed. "I guess I'm the one who's visiting, only I'm not, really." She followed the skunk into Brody's bedroom. Somehow it seemed a little safer with the animal there— especially since Brody said that Guinevere was de-scented and trained. De-scenting made a big difference, right there.

She spread up the bed—not all that carefully, either. And bent to pick up his dirty socks. Ugh. She should've brought rubber gloves. Just as she finished picking up the laundry,

Guinevere dashed under the bed and proceeded to make a big fuss in a cardboard box. Rita doubted that Brody would want his skunk to use that box for bathroom duty, so, on her hands and knees, she peered under. "Guinevere, come on out here!"

But the skunk showed no sign of giving up her box. Rita wondered what the appropriate skunk call was.

"Here, kitty-kitty." No, that didn't sound right. Maybe a dog command would work better. "Guinevere, come!"

No movement whatsoever. "Well, okay. I'll crawl under there and get you, then." She stretched with all her might and barely caught the corner of the box, then pulled it out, skunk and all. "Now, Guinevere, stop messing with me. I have to clean up this room."

She tossed the box on the bed, and a few letters flew out, along with the scent of cheap perfume. "Can't be you," she mumbled to the skunk. After glancing at a few of the return addresses, sparkly hearts, and perfume blotches, Rita realized that the entire box was full of fan mail—probably bucklebunnies he wanted to be able to contact.

The pink one on top beckoned her. What did these girls write? She'd never been so frivolous as to waste a perfectly good stamp on a good-looking, hard drinking, woman-chasing cowboy. She turned her head, but then had to look back again. Reading another person's mail was definitely wrong. She would never do such a thing.

Guinevere jumped back into the box and flipped the pink envelope onto the floor. Rita picked it up again. Scented. Maybe she could take a quick peek at the handwriting style. No, that would be wrong.

She opened it. And read it. And giggled.

"Listen to this, Guinny. 'I love your moves,'" she read with great drama. "'You're so dashing and daring! When you come back to Moses Lake, give me a call, and I'll show you my moves.' I'll bet she has moves." Rita giggled as she stuffed the letter back in its pink envelope and tossed it in the box.

The skunk dug out another letter, bright red, this time.

"Oh, no. I'm not reading another."

Guinevere shoved it closer to Rita.

"Nope. Not gonna do it." But the picture of the skunk under the return address got the better of her. "Okay, one more. But that's it. We put the box back under the bed."

She could have sworn the skunk nodded, then jumped in her lap and peered at the letter. "You like red, do you?" she asked as she slid the note out. "So do I, but don't tell anyone. I only wear earth tones at work. Actually, I hate them, but if you want to climb the corporate ladder, well, you wear earth tones."

The skunk patted the letter.

"Impatient little devil, aren't you?" She unfolded the letter and dumped red and silver glitter on her lap. Sighing, she wished the horny little witch had to clean it up herself. Whoever thought of the glitter-in-letters ought to be condemned to vacuum cleaner hell.

Clearing her throat, she put her best melodramatic flair into it. "Oh, Brody. You're sooooo handsome. Will you go out. . ."

"Anytime, darlin'."

Rita bolted straight in the air, glitter flying everywhere.

Chapter 5

I've got 'em now. With Brody's 'moves,' he'll certainly be able to make hay with this one. Ha! Rita fell right square into Guinevere's trap. A woman in love wants to know everything there is to know about her man, and Rita got a good dose of how many fillies are after hers.

Excellent plan I concocted, if I do say so myself.

Now maybe Brody will wake up to smell the coffee, er, perfume. Rita has the hots for him, I just know it. Never has he taken so long to get a filly into his bed. But then, none of the others were women that he wanted to keep for life. Not that he'd admit it.

Now, keep your hooves crossed. . .

Rita was so shocked she thought her teeth would melt together. "Brody Alexander, don't you go sneaking up on me. Ever!"

"Hell, walking into your own house isn't sneaking up. Didn't you hear the screen door slam?"

She hadn't. Her heart thumped and her stomach knotted. She burned with embarrassment. She had to get out of there, now, glitter or not. And she'd have a good talking-to with that darned skunk later.

"Uh, Phyllis has to go back to the diner." She hopped off the bed, upending the box of letters and knocking over the bag of dirty socks. Brushing past him, she made haste for the front door. "There won't be anyone to sit with Mom."

Her heart didn't stop thudding until she had hopped into the sanctuary of her earth tone Volvo, locked the doors, and started the engine. Brody stood in the doorway, waving and grinning. That man ought to be shot. She gunned the motor and tore down the driveway, kicking up a roostertail of dust.

The car bounced and jolted, but she pressed the accelerator harder. If she went fast enough, she'd only hit the tops of the bumps. She swung into the driveway, spraying gravel and fishtailing, then slid to a stop and ran into the house, straight into her room and slammed the door.

"Rita? Is that you?"

Her mom's voice echoed in her head. Answer her, you coward. But she could barely get her breath, let alone say anything. She gulped some air, leaned on the wall, and closed her eyes. Every affirmation she'd learned in management training taunted her.

She had done a bad thing.

"Rita?"

Taking one more deep breath, she said, "Yes, Mom, it's me. I'll be right out as soon as I change clothes." As if she needed to change clothes. She ripped off her blue t-shirt and put on a white one, then ran a brush through her hair.

She gazed into the mirror, and thank goodness she didn't look any different than she had before the dastardly deed she had so brazenly committed. Her scared-rabbit expression might be a dead giveaway, though.

With a smile on her face and her head held high, she ventured into her mother's bedroom. "All done."

"Already?" Her mom shook her head. "That didn't take long."

"Nope, Brody said he'd finish. I guess he had something to do and wanted me out of the way." Second sin of the day, she thought—lying to her mother. Complications were adding up fast.

Phyllis stashed the book she'd been reading in her purse. "I was about to go find out just who was in the house."

With a calm smile and a steady voice, Rita said, "I spilled something on my shirt." Sin number three.

"Well, Tommy and I best get back to the diner," Phyllis said as she closed her purse and put the strap over her shoulder. "Give me a call if you need anything. And stop by. I'll give you a free piece of apple pie—you're looking a little puny these days."

"I'll walk you out to the car."

"No." Judy pushed the blankets back. "I need to do business, and then I need my pain pills—and neither can wait one more minute." She patted Phyllis' arm. "Thanks, dear. We'll be in town for that pie in a few days."

Phyllis left while Rita helped Judy to the bathroom, and by her wan complexion, Rita could tell that her mom was, indeed, in pain. She sure hated to give her more of those pain pills, though, considering all the embarrassing things she'd said while under the influence.

"Only one pill," Rita said as she eased Judy back on the bed. "Two pills make you, uh, well, not yourself."

"I'm hurting, Rita."

"I'll give you one pill, and if the pain hasn't subsided in half an hour, I'll give you the second. How's that?"

"You better get me some crackers and 7-Up, too. My stomach's a little sour." She frowned and studied Rita. "Is that glitter in your hair?"

"Ye. . .uh, no, Mom, it's a new kind of hairspray." She hurried out of the room. Number four.

As Brody drove down the lane, he saw Phyllis' car and waved her over. She slowed her car to a stop and after the dust settled, they both rolled down their windows.

"Make it fast, handsome. I've got to get to the diner."

He chuckled at her ribbing. "Bring your boy and the others over to the practice pen tomorrow morning at ten, and I'll give 'em a show."

She pointed at the cast on his left arm. "You sure you ought to be doing that?"

"Hell, Phyllis, no one ever ought to fight bulls. It's just something we do. Besides, there's nothing wrong with my wheels. So bring the kids over. It'll only last half an hour or so, and you'll be able to get to the diner in time."

"Will do. See you tomorrow." She drove off.

He rolled his window up as fast as he could with his bum arm to keep the cloud of dust to a less than suffocating level and stepped on the accelerator.

Rita had given him an idea, but he didn't know how it would go over. And, he had to admit, his plan was a bit ornery. He pulled to a stop in front of her house, got out, then took the box of letters in his good arm.

"Hello, the house," he called out before he knocked on the door. That nicety was something he'd learned ten years ago when he first moved here—people wanted to know who'd come calling.

Rita opened the door. She took one look at the box, and slammed the door in his face.

"Rita! This isn't what you think. Let me in, please." He stood there for a considerable amount of time, listening to her bang pans around in the kitchen. He knocked again. "Rita, I've come to offer your mom a job."

More pan banging. Maybe even louder.

If he'd known that turning down her teenage advances would leave a lifelong grudge, he'd have let his baser instincts take over as they'd wanted to. "Rita, be reasonable."

The door opened, her eyes shooting sparks. "Reasonable? Reasonable?" She slammed the door so hard, the porch vibrated and a gust of wind ruffled his hair.

Okay, so she didn't want to be reasonable. He didn't, either, when he was around her. Without a second thought, he barged into the house.

Rita glared at him, tapping the broad side of a good-sized butcher knife in the palm of her hand. "One word, cowboy, and I'll cut your heart out."

"About what?" He wondered what had her in such a snit. "I

72

just wanted to pay Judy to send signed pictures to these young folks." Maybe she felt guilty about reading his fan mail without permission—but that certainly was a minor offense. Frankly, he didn't care who read it and the whole situation reminded him that he needed to get responses to the fans who were kind enough to write. Some of the letters had sat around for six months.

"Like I said, one word." She turned to the kitchen counter and murdered a tomato, guts splattering on the wall.

He hightailed into Judy's bedroom, thinking Rita wasn't too amenable to small talk right then.

"Hey, Judy. I brought you a chance to make a little money while you're laid up." He sat the box on the bed beside her. "How are you feeling today?"

"My knee hurts worse than yesterday."

He nodded. "Yeah, that's the way it goes. Always worse once the meds from the hospital completely wear off. But once you get through this mess, it'll all be worth it."

"Would you see if Rita forgot about my pain pill? Then we can talk about this project you've brought me."

He rubbed the back of his head as he walked slowly to the kitchen. Bad bulls, he could handle. Winter blizzards and drunk cowboys, no problem. Rita Markum, well, she was a force to be reckoned with. And he didn't feel like tangling with her at the moment. Or maybe he did, and that was his problem. He'd never been hot for an attached woman—at least, not that he'd ever known. And he wished he weren't now.

He stood quietly while she arranged a tray for Judy. She either hadn't noticed him or chose to ignore him on purpose. He cleared his throat. She flinched and spilled 7-Up on the tomato guts, then glared at him.

"What do you want?

"You're mom's ready for her pill."

"I know. I fixed her some lunch, er, dinner to go with it. The pills make her sick."

He noticed her lapse of terminology. The noon meal was lunch in the city, dinner out here. She had made the conversion to city life, he figured, even in her speech. He felt a little sad about that, because when the excitement wore off, she'd realize what she'd thrown away.

"Yeah, those pain pills are potent, all right. I'll tell her you're on your way."

Nodding, she went back to making salad as if he'd never come into the kitchen. He couldn't help notice her derriere movement that accompanied her vegetable chopping. Damn, she was pretty!

He moseyed back to Judy's room. "She's about done."

"Thanks." She pulled the box closer to her and took out a letter. "So what do you want me to do with these?"

"I have another box out in the pickup that I'll get in a minute. It's full of envelopes and my bullfighting pictures. I thought if you'd address the envelopes and hand them to me, I'll put their names on pictures and sign them. Then after I leave, you can stuff the envelopes and stamp them. Luke can bring it all back when he comes to get you for my practice show in the morning."

"What show?" Rita asked. She stood in the doorway, holding Judy's tray. "Mother, you're not going anywhere."

"Come here, kiddo," Judy said as she motioned for her daughter to come to her, "and give me my pill."

Rita set the tray on the bedstand. "It's noon now, so if you're still hurting at twelve-thirty, I'll bring another one."

Judy took the pill with water and handed the glass back to Rita. "Hand me a cracker, please. And the 7-Up."

"I brought a vegetable plate, too, and some French Onion dip."

Rita's tenderness with her mother's care brought a longing from deep inside Brody. Anyone could tell they enjoyed one another's company—not just the familial love he felt for his own mother. Truth be told, the whole community cared for one another, as evidenced by their desire to make a home for children whose own families couldn't care for them.

"What show?" Rita asked again.

"I'm having a show for the boys. Come on over and join the fun. It's just a rehearsal, really, since the animals haven't gone through their act for a week and a half. Plus, I'll be doing a little bullfighting just to make sure I'm up to snuff for the show next weekend."

"Another show?"

"Rodeo. I'm leaving a week from Thursday. I'll work Friday and Saturday nights, and I'll be back Sunday. Give Luke a call if you need anything—he hired a neighbor boy to do your mom's chores in the mornings and evenings."

Rita huffed up. "I can feed our animals. Fifty-three head of yearling beeves and a couple of horses don't amount to much work."

Brody cleared his throat to prevent a chuckle, figuring he was in enough hot water with her, although he still didn't know exactly why. He flashed his A-Number-One grin at her—known to devastate the most hardened of souls. "I know, but if you don't have to worry about the animals for a week, you can concentrate on getting Judy on her feet. I imagine she'll get a little cantankerous once she starts to feel better."

"I will not!" Judy sounded indignant, but she had a smile on her face. Rita, however, did not.

"You're already showing the signs." He stood. "Let's get to work on these letters. I'll get the rest of the stuff."

As he left, he heard Rita mutter, "I'd like to take care of an animal or two."

Or that's what he thought she said. He wondered why she was so adamant about feeding the livestock.

"You can feed the dog," he called over his shoulder.

When he came back, she handed him a bone.

Rita escaped into her bedroom—refuge of old and still as comforting. She flopped onto the bed facedown and pulled the pillow over the back of her head.

Even so, she still couldn't get Brody's swagger out of her mind. She rolled over, threw the pillow across the room, then watched it slide down the wall. Sighing, she went over and picked it up. She gave it a few good punches, but not too hard, since she didn't want to damage it.

That would be the topper to a perfect day—chasing feathers all over the house. It would go with the glitter. She went to the mirror and tried to see if any glitter remained on the top of her head. Darn, she'd lent her hand mirror to her mom, but Rita wasn't about to go get it. Straining her eyes, she bent her head down and looked up. Drat! She couldn't quite see the top of her head.

Then she tried it again, only faster. She couldn't see the crown of her head faster, either. Double damn! She couldn't take a shower right then, not with Studly in her mom's room, happily sending pictures to his fans. Of the female teen-bopper variety.

Finally, she bent over and brushed the heck out of her hair, red glitter flying in the air and settling on the dresser and floor. She'd vacuum glitter off the floor—and curtains, and walls, and bed—later, and probably for the next six weeks. Long weeks, with Brody showing up all the time.

She straightened and looked in the mirror, hoping the vigorous brushing removed most of the glitter from her hair. Hand addressing envelopes. She snorted. If Brody lived in the twenty-first century like everyone else, he'd enter the addresses on the computer and print labels. Then, he'd have a mailing list for . . . well, she didn't know what for, exactly, but he'd have one. Still, nobody hand-addressed envelopes these days.

She heard her mother calling, so she gave her hair another couple of swipes. "Coming." With any luck at all, Studly would be gone.

He wasn't. Sitting cross-legged on the floor, he used the chair for a desk and autographed eight-by-ten glossies with a red marker, writing the slogan, "Keep your head up and your feet down."

That piece of bullfighting advice was for nearly anyone, especially teenage girls, Rita thought. "What do you need, Mom?"

Judy continued addressing an envelope. "Since Brody's here, you might as well do the fitting so I can finish his costume before he leaves Thursday," she said without looking up. She licked a stamp, pasted it on the corner, and handed the envelope to Brody. "I would have done it last week, but I couldn't get him to hold still long enough."

Rita had sincerely hoped her mom would forget about the stupid fitting. Why, she'd have to put her hands—well, lots of places. Besides, she was lousy at it—sewing, that is.

Brody autographed a picture and stuffed it into the envelope Judy had addressed, then twisted around to look at Rita. "I'll hold real still." He raised one eyebrow and grinned. "Are you ready?"

She'd rather face a firing squad. "Sure."

Brody had been in some strange situations since he went on the road as a bullfighter, but not as strange as this. He stood still as a boulder while the woman of his dreams kneeled in front of him, adjusting the crotch of his baggies. But he dared not think about where her hands were.

Judy watched every move Rita made on the pretense of telling her how the adjustments should be pinned, but he didn't believe that for a minute. Judy was there to make good and sure Brody kept his hands off her daughter while Rita had her hands all over him.

And boy, did she. She rested her wrist on his inner thigh while she pinned.

He silently recited the prologue to Canterbury Tales in Middle English, concentrating on combining the French and Germanic pronunciations, throwing in a little Celt for good measure.

Whan that aprill with his shoures soote
The droghte of march hath perced to the roote...

But the elevator went up a couple of floors in spite of his efforts. He wished she'd move her wrist. No, he wished . . . Damn! He studied the three bug carcasses in the overhead light, and concentrated on Chaucer:

And bathed every veyne in swich licour
Of which vertu engendred is the flour;

She slid her hand down his left leg, pleating the material as she went. But as the pants got tighter—well, the pants got a lot tighter higher up. No virtue whatsoever was engendered in his flower. But he bet there was a lot of sweet liqueur in hers.

Ah, double damn! He stared at the light again. The bug body on the right looked like a dragonfly. The left one, too. They probably fried while they were mating. . . How long could it possibly take to fit a pair of baggies?

He watched her clench the straight pins in her mouth while she began to go through the same procedure on is right leg. He closed his eyes and clenched his teeth as the back of her hand rustled against his groin.

Whan zephirus eek with his sweete breeth
Inspired hath in every holt and heeth
Tendre croppes, and the yonge sonne
Hath in the ram his halve cours yronne. . .

He'd like to ram his—

She jabbed him.

He jumped and grunted, then grabbed her wrist. "That was a might too close to the jewels, darlin'." His arousal was more than apparent, and not more than six inches from her face. Which aroused him more. Hell, he couldn't help it. He let go of her.

She looked him square in the eye and jabbed him again.

"What am I, your personal voodoo doll?"

Taking the last pin out of her mouth, she deftly slid it through the fold of material bunched between his legs. "No, just a prick."

Rita had been in uncomfortable situations before, but pinning up britches on a man with a boner—while her own mother watched—was definitely the worst. Did the man have no control?

About as much as she had, considering the stirrings deep in her abdomen. At least hers didn't show. Brody's arousal was all too evident, and she couldn't get away from it until she finished pinning. She considered jabbing him again, but he didn't deflate the first two times so she doubted a third poke would do the job.

"Mark the back pockets with chalk," her mother instructed. "We'll put Velcro on them to attach the scarves."

Rita inserted the last inseam pin. "Why not just sew them on?"

"In case he gets hooked, or close to it, the scarves won't hang him up."

Sounded logical. What didn't make sense was running in front of a bull in the first place. No, she didn't believe that—she'd always loved rodeo—she just didn't want to be involved with a man who thought putting himself in extreme danger was fun.

At least now she could get her face away from the tent in his pants. She retrieved the sewing basket and dug out some dressmaker's chalk, then drew a little square on each muscular hip. "How short do you want your britches?" she asked Brody.

"A couple of inches above my knees."

She knew that if his pants were too short, they wouldn't have enough movement to attract a bull, and if they were too long, they prevented his full range of motion. Exhaling a deep breath, she marked the hemline in four places on each pant leg.

Tossing the chalk and excess pins in the basket, she looked up at Brody. "All done."

He couldn't know how done, either. The whole process had been a trial for her—more than an engaged woman should have to endure.

He looked down at her and grinned. "Is that glitter in your hair?"

Rita tensed, her face on fire.

"No," her mom said, "it's hairspray."

Brody settled down to a nice cup of coffee while Rita fussed in the kitchen. She seemed nervous. Why, he couldn't say— he'd been the one put through trial by fire.

At the scratching on the screen door, Rita nodded toward it. "Let Beauty in, will you?"

But when he opened it, not only did Beauty stand there, tail wagging, but also Guinevere, Perseus, and Socrates—all looking quite guilty for some reason. "What are you guys doing here? Go home!"

Perseus circled three times and lay down, tucking his head under one paw. Guinevere hid behind him. Socrates' ears perked up at the ringing of the telephone. So did Brody's when he heard Rita say, "Hi, David. How'd it go?"

The animals could wait. For now, he wanted to see if his mother had done what he'd instructed.

Rita stood at the sink, the cordless phone tucked between her ear and shoulder while she peeled a cucumber. He strained to hear David's words, but they were unintelligible. She dropped the peeler and the cucumber and whirled around toward Brody, her lovely shaped eyebrow raised in alarm. "France!"

He wondered if this had anything at all to do with his instructions to his mother. Obviously, she had found another position for David rather than the one at headquarters. Rita paced back and forth, still listening. "But France?" She backed up to the counter and leaned on her elbow, still holding the phone to her ear.

"You could turn down the promotion."

Barely able to keep from hollering and slapping his knee, he silently congratulated his mother for getting rid of David so handily. But then he remembered that breaking Rita's heart had never been his goal—he'd only wanted her to get the position she deserved. Still, if she and David were truly committed to one another, they'd find a way to be together.

"But David, what about my job? I can't just leave it. And what about the house? It's not built yet, but we do have a monster mortgage."

Brody wondered if his mother knew how Rita would handle this situation. Probably yes, and there was probably a notepad with *Rita* on the front of it.

"The company's buying it?" Rita quit pacing and plopped into a chair. "You're on your way here?" She jammed her fingers in her hair and squeezed her eyes shut. "Good, because we need to talk."

She stood and slammed the phone back on the charger, then turned to Brody, her eyes blazing. "Pettybottham Enterprises has just ruined my life. So much for the benevolent company image."

He had to know why. "But I've always heard they're a great place to work."

"They were. Until now." She attacked the cucumber with the peeler.

"And?"

"David's been promoted—and moved to the Paris office."

Now it was Brody's turn to frown, since he'd told his mother that Rita was the one who deserved a promotion. At least David hadn't been placed at the Houston office. "I thought that's what you wanted? The promotion for your boyfriend, I mean."

"In *Seattle*, not *France!*"

Glancing at the screen door, Brody saw all four animals peering in, ears perked. Bunch of eavesdroppers. He could have sworn he detected a smile from that crazy mule.

The phone rang again, and Rita jumped to grab it. "Hello?"

Expecting another call from David, Brody was surprised when she said, "She's fine, Miss Pettybottham. Thanks for asking."

What the hell was his sister doing calling here?

"Of course we'd love to have you visit. Funding the children's home is our primary concern." Rita's gaze glanced about the room as if sizing up its condition.

Brody rolled his eyes. Caroline was coming *here*? Now he felt a major headache coming on. The last thing he wanted was for his talkative sister to come to Owyhee County and ruin the life he'd built. No one would ever treat him like a normal rancher again once they learned he owned seventy-five percent of a Fortune 500 corporation. He had to get on the phone and stop her.

"I've gotta go," he mumbled.

Chapter 6

Oh, the look on Brody's face when he realized that Darling David would soon be out of the picture! Of course, my human still doesn't know why he's relieved—that's for more reasonable species to cogitate. But then, a more reasonable species doesn't need to cogitate on the obvious.

I had a hunch after Rita tore out of Brody's house like her britches were on fire that there'd be something interesting happening at her house. It seemed well worth the three-mile trek for Perseus, Guinevere, and me. Talk about pay off!

Anyway, this makes my job much easier, even if Mr. Perfect will be making one more appearance. I've always known that Rita would never agree to Brody's advances until she's free to do so, even if it meant spending a lifetime of unhappiness. Humans have such crazy notions sometimes.

Now, to make her see Truth. Yes, I have another idea that will seal the deal for sure. Throw a little salt over your withers and let's get to work.

The last place Rita wanted to drive was back to Brody's place, glitter or not, but her mom insisted she needed to get out of the house. Getting Judy to the car—crutches and all—was somewhat of a tussle, but they managed.

"Phyllis and the boys will be there," Judy had argued, which made plenty enough people to distract Rita from. . .well, thinking about *him*.

Brody's image erased all logical thought and she hit a rut a little too fast.

Judy grunted and protectively held her knee, the pillow between her knee and the door cushioning the blow. "Take it easy, honey."

"Sorry, Mom." Rita slowly pulled the Volvo into Brody's driveway, avoiding as many ruts as possible for her mother's sake, and parked the car close to the crude grandstand next to the round pen, then waited for the dust to settle before opening the car door.

"Luke should've hosed down the dirt," Rita said, not only to make conversation, but to see her mom's reaction to Luke's name.

Judy chuckled and peered through the window, probably in search of the outlaw in question. "There's not enough water in Owyhee County to keep this dust down—it's a losing proposition."

"I hope those benches hold together," Rita remarked, really meaning it this time.

Judy smiled. "Oh, they will. Luke built them last year. They're not pretty, but they do the trick."

Her mom practically sang Luke's name. Considering she'd been preaching the *No Cowboys* rule for a quarter of a century, she sure spent a lot of time thinking about the old bullrider. Worse, she'd gotten testy when Rita called her on it.

Speaking of the devil, Luke knocked on Judy's window."

"Looks like your boyfriend's here, Mom. Let's get you out of this car."

Not that Rita had much to do, since Luke had already opened the passenger door and was lifting Judy out of the car. And maybe even sneaking in a little kiss, although Rita couldn't quite tell for sure. Her mom sure wrapped her arms around his neck fast enough. Somehow Rita had a feeling it was for more than just to make certain she didn't fall.

Luke spread his jacket on the bench. "This'll keep the stickers out of your tush, Sugar."

"Thanks, although with the drugs they have me on, I'm not sure I'd even feel it." Her mother giggled as Luke helped her to the bench. Rita more than suspected that if hanky-panky hadn't already happened, it would soon. If it did, she didn't want to know about it. She shuddered at the thought of her own mother having s-e-x, then felt a little silly for being such a prude.

"In that case, I'll use my Dawg cushion." Rita fetched her University of Washington Huskies stadium seat from the trunk. From the corner of her eye, she saw Brody jump on the fence of the holding pen just in back of the round pen and stand, balanced, on the top rail. The bulls milled around, blowing snot and kicking up dirt. She tried not to look, but finally caved and gave him the once-over. Twice.

Especially when he did a backflip off the fence and started his warm-ups.

Rita couldn't deny it—Brody Alexander cut a fine figure of a man as he flexed and stretched his muscles in preparation for the short bullfighting show. He had drawn a big red smile over his white greasepaint. A red-striped shirt covered his protective vest that made him look like a barrel, but couldn't hide his muscular shoulders.

She pulled her gaze away from him and sighed. "Don't you just love the smell of freshly disked earth?" she mused out loud, hoping she made it seem as if she hadn't been ogling Brody. Luke had watered and worked the ground in the round pen until the top four inches of dirt was spongy enough to absorb shock and help prevent injuries.

But the red tights over Brody's powerful legs held her attention even more. The memory of fitting his new pair of baggy denim shorts made her blush. It hadn't taken her long to make the alterations and sew the Velcro for the handkerchiefs trailing from his hip pockets. Luke had been all too happy to come over and pick up the baggies. . .and chat with her mom awhile.

A battered green derby scrunched over his ears, and in Rita's mind, crowned Brody king of bullfighters.

She tried to ignore him, although she had to concentrate to

keep from looking. A couple of bulls snorted and pawed in the holding pen, waiting for action. The air tingled with anticipation and bit of anxiety.

As she fussed with the pillow covering the log in front of the bench where her mother sat, Rita was determined not to look at him again. She gently elevated Judy's leg.

Judy gave her an inquisitive stare, then sighed. "For the third time, Rita, I'll be perfectly all right."

Luke ran a big brindle brahma-cross into the holding pen with a couple of other bulls. Rita nudged her mother. "You're supposed to be watching the show, not the foreman."

"Hrmph, I'm just waiting for Phyllis. She's bringing Tommy and the other kids, you know." She patted the bench beside her. "Sit down. Once we get home, you'll have to get busy cleaning. Miss Pettybottham will be here mid afternoon, and your young man should arrive early evening. You might as well relax while you can."

On cue, Phyllis drove up. Before the dust settled, Tommy and four other boys scrambled out of the old Pontiac—Tommy being the smallest, and the biggest boy probably not more than six or seven. Phyllis pointed toward the bench. "You boys sit down and behave yourselves now. The first one that disobeys Brody sits in the car for the rest of the show."

As if deaf, they all took off with wide grins on their faces and sparkles in their eyes and headed straight for the object of their adoration. Rita had always been amazed at his way with children. They all loved Brody.

He greeted them with high-fives. "Howdy, boys. You all ready for a show?"

After they nodded, he said, "You know the rules—one, sit on the bench and stay there, and two, holler as loud as you can. These bulls need to get used to lots of noise. Think you can do that?"

"Yes, sir!" they chimed, then, as a pack, ran to the bench, kicking up dirt as they slid to a stop in front of the bench. One boy pointed to Judy's leg and looked at her admiringly. "Wow, did a bull hook you?"

"Nope," Tommy said, taking his thumb out of his mouth. "She gots cut on at the doctor so she'll be all better. Mom says she'll be kickin' butt in no time."

"Tommy!" Phyllis clapped her hand to her forehead.

Judy chuckled. "Sit down, boys. Brody's about ready to start the show."

"And if you're all good," Phyllis added, "I have cinnamon rolls and milk for afterwards." That did the trick. The boys instantly plopped down and waited for Luke to run out the first bull.

"I'm ready," Brody called. "Are you all ready?"

"YES!" all five of the boys chorused.

"Okay, Luke, let that little yellow bull in. I'll warm up with him." He turned back to the boys. "This first one's named June Bug because he was born in June and he's small as bulls go, only weighing about twelve-hundred pounds, but he's fast and he enjoys hooking bullfighters who aren't looking."

Rita sucked in her breath as the bull pounded the earth behind Brody. He still hadn't turned around. She jumped up in a sweat. "Watch out!"

Brody whirled, slapped the bull on the side of the head, and spun him around. The bull pawed and snorted as the bullfighter teased him. With a shake of his head, June Bug took after Brody, who ran across the arena and hopped up to the top rail of the fence.

Rita plopped back on the bench, flushed with embarrassment.

As the bull got to the fence, Brody dove off and, using June Bug's horns for leverage, did a one-armed handspring across the bull's back with the grace any gymnast would be proud of. Rita cringed at the pain that move must have caused as he pulled his sleeve back down over the cast on his left arm.

The boys cheered wildly, and Rita discovered herself shouting as loudly as they were. Brody doffed his hat at her, then allowed June Bug to chase him out of the round pen, the boys laughing uproariously. But while Brody ran up on the gate, Luke opened it and June Bug seemed quite happy to return to the holding pen, although he still shook his horns and snorted for a bit.

"I think you boys liked that a little more than June Bug did." After the laughter died down, Brody nodded to Luke. "I'll have the brangus next." Turning back to his small audience, he said, "This next bull is a muley and weighs eighteen-hundred pounds—pretty good sized."

"He ain't no mule," Tommy muttered, frowning. "Socrates is a mule." He stuck his thumb back in his mouth.

Rita gave him a little hug. "Muley means he doesn't have any horns."

"That's right," Brody said, winking at Rita. "All right now, I'm going to show you footwork on this one. His name is Johnny Ringo. He's big, but he's fast. I can't be bigger or faster, but I can be smarter."

Rita wasn't so sure about that as the mottled brown and black bull ran into the round pen. She noticed that Brody didn't turn his back on the huge animal this time. But he made a believer out of her as he darted and dodged the snorting, bellowing bull. Brody's grace and confidence showed beyond a shadow of a doubt that rodeoing ran through his blood.

"Good, ain't he?" Phyllis beamed at him as brightly as the five little boys sitting beside her. They all had a serious case of hero worship—not undeserved, either.

"Very." In the face of danger, Brody was happier than Rita had seen him since the last time she'd seen him fight bulls ten years ago.

She'd known men like him all her life. Heck, her father had been a bullrider. These men would endure painful injuries, hours and hours of driving, peanut butter and jelly sandwiches for days, and sleeping eight or ten men to a room just to pay for a chance to ride or fight a bull. Few people out of the rodeo business had any inkling how truly tough cowboys were.

But she knew, and she knew what years of such a bone-crunching life would do to a healthy human body. That's why she lived smack-dab in the middle of Seattle—to avoid the heartache of watching someone you love slowly destroy himself.

Her Seattle friends would think Brody was bonkers for working while he was still mending. They'd think her mom was, too, for not following doctor's orders. Rita agreed—her mother should be home and in bed—or in an easy chair with her leg propped up—but Rita knew it was almost a badge of courage to be up and about if a body had a single breath left in it, and her mom was a product of her upbringing.

Phyllis gave Judy the thumbs-up. "It's good to see you up and about." She hunkered down and giggled as if she had a juicy bit of gossip. "I sent another bucklebunny to Triangle this morning. Classy broad, though. Had on a business suit. But she couldn't fool old Phyllis, especially when I asked her if she was here to visit Brody and she said 'not this time' as if she'd made a regular habit of it." She winked at Rita. "So when she asked for directions, I done sent her up to Triangle same's all the others."

Judy shook her head once. "Tch, I wonder if there'll ever be an end to the stream of women pounding on his door."

"A bucklebunny in a business suit?" Rita pondered out loud, then sucked in her breath in a flash of panic. "Oh, no! I bet that was Caroline Pettybottham who disperses the funds from MOMMI. Remember, I applied for a grant for the children's home."

With widened eyes and a wrinkled brow, Phyllis whispered, "Oh, cripes. Do you know what she looks like?"

"No, but she's visiting this afternoon—her plane's due in anytime now. Maybe she took an earlier flight. Was this woman driving a rental car?"

Shaking her head, Phyllis smirked. "Don't know—it was one of them big boats. Lincoln, maybe. Black. But if she *is*

Caroline Pettybottham, we sure won't get any money out of her now."

Rita jumped up. "We've got to go get her!"

Judy tugged her daughter's arm. "Sit down. You'll distract Brody. Fifteen minutes isn't going to make a bit of difference."

Brody noticed the women whispering instead of watching the show. Actually, he noticed Rita whispering instead of watching him, and that was not his plan. Well, she'd pay attention on this next one.

"Let out Owyhee Thunder, Luke," he called, then turned to his small audience. "This bruiser is a champion bull on the Northwest Rodeo Circuit, but he's a bit tubby, so we brought him back home to put him on a diet." Phyllis and Luke were the only ones laughing. "He's half Charolais and half Brahma. Let's see what he can do."

Brody did a little fancy footwork, loving the sounds of the boys' ooo's and ahhhs, then got a laugh out of them by snagging his green derby on one of the bull's horns. For the grand finale, he teased the bull into charging, then did a handspring over the bull's head and walked the length of his back, jumping off the tail end.

"That's it, kids," he said, never letting the bull out of his line of sight. "We'll have another show in a few weeks."

The boys stood and cheered as Brody herded Owyhee Thunder back into the holding pen. Brody thought Rita even cracked a smile.

As he leapt the corral fence to talk to them, Luke hollered, "Run! Bull's out!"

Brody ran full tilt to the kids. "Get in the car! NOW." They dove in, Tommy with the help of Phyllis' boot, and Phyllis on top of the boys with the help of Brody's track shoe. He barely got the door closed before dodging the charging bull, who stopped, snorting and pawing, and glared at Phyllis and the kids through the half-open window.

"Start the car and get the hell out of here!" Brody waved a

red handkerchief to catch Owyhee Thunder's attention.

Phyllis managed to wiggle over the seat backs to the driver's seat and start the car. With the sound of the engine, the bull backed off, but then headed straight toward Rita who struggled to help Judy stand with the aid of her crutches. The beast charged the ladies from the direction of their car, so they had to hustle in the other direction, although Judy's hustle was severely impaired, and that put Rita in mortal danger as well.

Taking his only chance, Brody dashed into harm's way, grabbed the bull by the ear and hollered to get the animal's attention. Owyhee Thunder wheeled around, snot flying.

Brody couldn't dodge fast enough. The violent impact of the bull's head on his shorts sent him flying high, and all he could do was try to position himself so he'd hit the ground running. Instead, he fell flat on his back and lost every molecule of wind in his lungs.

Desperate for air, he sprang to his feet.

Owyhee Thunder charged the two women as Brody wheezed. From nowhere, Luke swooped Judy, crutches and all, in his arms and ran for the house. Rita stood alone, wide-eyed and frozen in place. "Climb the fence!" Brody hollered, hoping to shock her back into action. "I'll get him turned."

Still, she didn't move. He struggled to gulp more air, then ripped the other handkerchiefs from his hip pockets. While the bull pawed the ground, staring at Rita, Brody darted to the bull's side and draped the cloths over the snorting animal's eyes. "Run, Rita! Run NOW."

Perseus yipped with excitement. Luke must have let the dog out of the house. A performing animal, he was rarely around the cattle, but he was a natural born herder and this time he'd earn his dog biscuits.

Brody pointed toward the barn. "Perseus, take him that way."

The dog ran behind the bull and nipped him in the hock. Owyhee Thunder bucked, nearly kicking Perseus in the head, but the near miss didn't dampen the Australian Shepherd's enthusiasm.

Brody used the diversion to pick up Rita, throw her over his shoulder, and run full-steam for the house. "I thought you were a country girl," he said as he put her down just inside the door."

Pale and drawn, she opened her mouth as if to say something, but nothing came out except a croak.

"Sit in the livingroom with your mom and have some coffee," he told her. He wanted to kiss her quivering lips, but still had a bull to corral and a dog to keep safe. "I'll be back in a minute."

Perseus hopped back and forth barking happily at Owyhee Thunder—the dog was at his glory. Brody exhaled some serious tension. The bull stood at the gate chewing his cud, but Perseus obviously thought he'd caught the Big One. Brody whistled and pointed to the house. Reluctantly, the dog went in, tail between his legs, moping every step of the way, but as soon as he stepped onto the porch he assumed the air of victor.

After the bull ambled placidly back into the corral, swishing his tail at a bothersome fly, Brody dashed into the house. Luke tended to Judy on the loveseat, while Rita sat on the couch, sipping a cup of coffee as if nothing had happened.

"Good show," she said without looking up. "A little exciting at the end."

He sagged onto the opposite end of the couch, his hopes that he had impressed her dashed. He'd never tried to impress a woman before and now he knew why. "A little."

She put her coffee mug on the end table and stood. "We have a problem."

Raising his hand, palm out, he said, "I'll put a double gate up so that won't happen again."

"I know you'll take care of the safety issue, that's not what I'm talking about. The difficulty is the funding for the children's home."

Brody couldn't believe his ears. "You've just been threatened by two-thousand pounds of angry bull, and you're worried about money?"

"No, I'm worried about Caroline Pettybottham."

"She can't be that bad. Just talk to her."

"That's still not the problem. Phyllis sent her to Triangle."

Brody nearly choked just thinking about his prissy sister driving on that washed-out, one-lane country road. "Triangle? Why in tarnation would she do that?"

"Because she thought Miss Pettybottham was one of your little bucklebunnies hoping for a ride," she said righteously. "Phyllis sends them all to Triangle."

He sighed, pleading with the Big Bullfighter in the Sky for protection against all well-intentioned women.

"She's driving a Lincoln, Phyllis thinks."

"Zero ground clearance," he muttered. "Dagnabit, what was she thinking?" He headed for the bedroom to change clothes, and called over his shoulder, "We'll take my rig. Be ready."

"I'll drive your mother home and put her to bed," Luke said as he rose from the loveseat and handed Judy's crutches to her.

Rita rolled her eyes, not wanting to even think her mother was involved with another busted-up cowboy, even though Luke had never been anything but chivalrous. Her mom talked one way, but she acted quite the opposite. "Be sure that's all you do."

Judy pointed a crutch at her. "Rita!"

Luke chuckled and helped Judy to her feet, easing a crutch under each arm. "We'll be waiting for you. I'll get your livestock fed before you get back."

"That's not necessary," Rita protested. "I can do it myself."

"You could, but they'll get fed twice if you do."

Judy giggled as she hobbled out of the house. "You might as well give up, Rita. Luke can be stubborn as a mule when he wants to be."

After Luke followed Judy out of the house, Rita muttered, "You mean *all* men, *all* the time." And speaking of mules, old

93

Socrates wrote the song on stubbornness. Yep, the *Mule Blues*.

Brody came out of the bedroom buckling his belt. "What did you say?"

"Nothing."

Socrates peered through the door at her and half-neighed, half-brayed.

"Oh, shut up," she grumped.

"Huh?" Brody jammed on his Stetson and grabbed his keys. "Let's go."

As soon as Rita hopped into the pickup, Guinevere bolted out of the house and jumped on her lap. "Does this skunk really have to go?"

He shrugged. "Why not? She's been locked in the house all day." No sooner had he said that when Perseus bounded in the back seat and, panting excitedly with his slobbery tongue hanging out, rested his head over Rita's shoulder. She blew the lock of hair on her forehead, then, after a moment's hesitation, scratched his ears. "All right, boy. You can go, too."

Beauty whined and gazed mournfully at Brody. Rita winced, then nodded at him, so he let her dog into the backseat, too, saying, "I guess we might as well take the whole gang."

The mule stood by the driver's side door looking ever so forlorn. "Sorry, Socrates, but I'm not going to hitch up the trailer. We need to get going." The mule gave him a little nip on the arm and plodded off dejectedly.

"He hates to miss anything."

"Sometimes I could swear he understands everything we say," she said as she batted the skunk tail from her face—Caroline Pettybottham undoubtedly wouldn't be so accommodating. "Now that we have most of the menagerie, let's get going."

A few miles down the road she asked, "So where will we put Caroline if she needs a ride? Phyllis said her car was a huge luxury car—the worst choice for this country. It'll definitely bottom out, and could break an axle or tear off the oil pan if she's not careful. Do you think she'd get out and walk?"

"Not my si—uh, any city girl I ever knew." He frowned and rubbed his hand over the stubble on his chin. "Don't worry about it. If she can't follow us in her car, we'll put the animals in the camper and she can ride in the backseat."

What a mortifying thought. She could just imagine Miss Caroline Pettybottham, executor of MOMMI and sister of one of the richest men in America, with her perfect business suit and manicured nails covered with skunk and dog hair. "Oh, no. I need to make a good impression on this woman. She's made it quite clear that we had no business applying for funding without state certification, so I'm already on shaky ground."

"You'll be fine."

She pursed her lips at his patronizing tone. He didn't know how hard it was to get funding, and Phyllis, in her goodhearted way, had really made a mess just when things were looking up with MOMMI. Having already blown it once with Miss Pettybottham, Rita didn't look forward to the aftermath of this little rescue operation.

At least the skunk and the dogs were finally more interested in the passing scenery than in smothering her.

"There's the turn-off." She braced herself as Brody turned from the highway to the country road, carefully guiding the tires onto the high side of the ruts.

"Fresh tire tracks," he noted. "Not too many people are daring enough to take this road, so it looks like we'll be finding your funding source soon."

She crossed her arms over her bosom and frowned. "You don't have to sound so darned coldhearted about it."

After half an hour of road that rattled the fillings in her teeth, they finally came upon a black Lincoln Town Car wedged crossways on the lane. At least, it had probably started out as black. It was currently so covered with alkali dust that it looked tan with black speckles.

"Yo-boy," she murmured. "This is not gonna be good."

Brody chuckled, and patted her on the hand. "She's human,

I'm sure."

"One mad human, I'm sure."

As they drove up, a woman in a tan skirt and jacket got out of the car and slammed the door so hard that dust engulfed her in a cloud. She waved one hand while she cupped the other over her nose as she trudged to the pickup.

"Thank you for stopping, sir." Then she widened her eyes and glared at him.

"Didn't have much choice, ma'am."

Rita clobbered him in the ribs. "Brody Alexander!" Then she clambered out and circled in front of the vehicle, offering her hand. "Miss Pettybottham?"

"That would be me."

"I'm Rita Markum. Please join us." She cocked her head toward her smart-mouthed driver. "Don't mind him. He's a rodeo clown—need I say more?"

To her relief, Miss Pettybottham smiled. "No, Miss Markum, you needn't say a word more. Please call me Caroline—I'm sure we'll be seeing more of each other."

"Please remove those animals from the vehicle," Caroline huffed, hands on hips. Brody marveled at his sister's audacity here in the high mountain desert. Here, a person lived by the land's rules, not the other way around.

Rita opened the pickup door. Perseus soared out, dancing about Brody and barking with sheer joy. Forlornly, Beauty studied the ground, then plopped down and plodded away from the dust cloud. Guinevere daintily hopped onto the running board, then, hesitantly to the powdery earth, flicking the dust off her tail.

"A skunk!" Caroline let out a screech that could be heard for miles and leapt into the pickup, slamming the door and locking it.

Brody patted the top of the insulted skunk's head. "Don't mind her, Guinevere. Caroline's always been a coward." After he put the animals in the camper, Brody knocked on the passenger window and shouted, "She's a highly trained animal. De-scented."

Rolling down the window, Caroline raised her perfectly tweezed eyebrows. "I suppose you think that makes me happy."

He grinned, beating off the temptation to tease his bedraggled sister who, for the first time in her entire life, was covered in dust. She looked rather cute that way.

"Brody," Rita growled quietly with clenched teeth. "The children's home needs this woman's good graces, so behave."

"Yes, ma'am." He hadn't had such a good time with his sister in years, if ever.

"Oh, this is so disgusting!" Caroline groused, patting her clothes, trying to repair what seemed to be beyond redemption. Only a shower and a dry cleaner would be her salvation. The shower she could get, but he had a small bit of satisfaction that the nearest dry cleaner was a good two-hour drive from there— in the opposite direction as her destination.

"Do you have any bags?" Rita asked.

"Oh yes, I nearly forgot. There are three suitcases in the trunk and my briefcase in the front."

Brody jumped out of the pickup. "Where are the keys?"

"In the ignition. I didn't think anyone would be stealing a car stuck on a dreadful road in the middle of nowhere."

He nodded at Rita. "You get the briefcase and I'll get the bags." He didn't want her talking with Caroline until he could get his sister alone to establish a few ground rules. And find out why the hell she'd come here in the first place. It certainly had nothing to do with MOMMI—that check had already been cut.

The only other reason she could be here would be to interfere with his life, and he wouldn't be one bit surprised if his mother wasn't spearheading another one of her schemes to get him back into the corporate fold. In fact, he'd be astounded if she weren't.

But he would win this round, just like always.

Caroline had never seen so much of nothing in her life. Brody pulled the truck into Rita's driveway. The house was clean, but much too small, and the barn could use some repair and a new coat of paint. Everything within fifty miles had a coating of dust, including her. Why on God's green earth did her brother tolerate and even enjoy these conditions?

She wrinkled her nose as the animals ran off to relieve themselves. How people could live with these creatures was beyond her. A little donkey-horsey animal grazed nearby, lifting his head and looking at her. She inched nearer her brother just in case the wild animal went berserk. "I'll stay a few minutes and then I'll want to go to the hotel."

Her brother grinned, eyes twinkling. She remembered that look—he'd had the same expression when he'd filled her Barbie house with lizards and grasshoppers.

"If you wanted to stay in a hotel, you should've stayed in Boise, or at least Nampa. Grasmere, or the county seat, Murphy, for that matter, doesn't have any hotels."

She scanned the countryside, seeing nothing but the endless sagebrush and relentless dust. "What a dreadful place. I can't imagine what you see in it."

Shrugging, he said, "You wouldn't. Now, do you want me to carry your bags into Mrs. Markum's house, or not?"

"It seems like a terrible imposition."

"It is. She just had surgery on her knee. Her daughter is here for a few weeks to help out, though, so if you don't mind doing a few dishes and your own laundry, you'll be plenty welcome."

She'd never done either in her life and he knew it. Nevertheless, she had a job to do and she was determined to see it through. "All right then, if they invite me, I'll stay. But leave the bags in the truck for now. I don't want them to think me presumptuous."

"It's a little late for that. Why don't you just tell me what you're up to and be on your way. Mother has some sort of plan up her sleeve again, doesn't she?"

"Don't be a clod. You hired me to administer the MOMMI

funds, then you order me to cut a check for an application that's patently unfounded, albeit well-written, and you wonder why I want to know what's going on? That takes a lot of nerve, *Broderick Pettybottham.*"

"Do *not* call me that."

"Then don't expect me to go along with your little charade unless you humor me." She smiled smugly, knowing she had him there. She glanced at the dirty SUV parked in front of the house. "At least she has a decent car."

"That's not hers. It's a rental. Must be. . .damnation! Not that bloodsucker again."

She brightened. Maybe this day wasn't for naught, after all. "What bloodsucker?"

"One of our Pettybottham managers. David Parr."

"Is that so?" Her mother had emailed Mr. Parr's photograph and told her all about Miss Markum's fiancé. The mission: remove him and use Rita to lure Broderick back to the Texas office. This would be a much simpler task than she'd thought.

She hadn't played the seduction game for months.

Chapter 7

What a spirited filly! Brody's sister, that is. I had to get a good look at her so I hung out at the Markums', and she didn't disappoint me. She wore a fashionably short, tastefully tailored skirt and jacket, and her blonde hair was chopped in that current style where it looks like she got it cut with a chainsaw. I would never let anyone do such an abomination to my mane or tail, believe me. But I'm sure she thinks it's beautiful.

Anyway, Perseus could barely contain his anxiety when he reported back. He's worried that Miss Pettybottham is here to take her brother back to Texas. Now I don't mind telling you, it's too blasted hot in that part of the country. My ears wilt every time we have to go down there for a show.

Both Perseus and Guinevere gave the impression that Miss Pettybottham doesn't like them, and we'd end up having to train new humans. That, of course, is patently unacceptable.

My friends were quite interested in the other new arrival, though. It seems as though the interloper, David, just can't seem to stay away. He's back in Grasmere. Guinevere actually had a good idea. If we hook up David and Miss Pettybottham, we could get rid of two nuisances at once. This time I'll go along with their plan. It couldn't hurt, and it might help.

Meantime, I saw Rita stealing glances at Brody several times. And at the bullfighting show for the kids, she was downright enthralled. Rightfully so, I might add. So things are looking up there. Wedding arrangements are in order, and I have a plan to get things rolling.

I have no doubt that we'll see some Brodiettes soon. I hope so, because my human is becoming increasingly agitated. Not

that another human would notice, but we mules are exceedingly perceptive about these matters.
Okay, let's go to it.

Rita couldn't believe her bad luck. She'd hurried into the house the minute Brody stopped the pickup because the rental car parked in front of the house could be only one person— David. He'd arrived early.

"Miss Caroline Pettybottham is coming in, David," she said without so much as a greeting. "Our discussion about your offer will have to wait."

"It's not an offer, it's a done deal. I'm moving to France as soon as I get my passport and paperwork in order. It's a chance of a lifetime. I studied French for three years in college, you know."

Her heart felt like an anvil, weighing down her chest. She wanted to scream, or maybe to slap the matter-of-fact expression off David's face. All that work, all her careful plans, and poof! Gone. Instead of garroting him, she took a breath and chose her words carefully.

"So I'm out of the picture."

"No. The Paris assignment only lasts three years and then I'll be moved somewhere else—maybe even back to Seattle. We could get married then."

"Or not?"

He shrugged. "Or not."

"Why are you even here, then?"

"There were a few additions that corporate wanted made on the report. I thought you could do them up tonight so I could get back to Seattle tomorrow."

"You *thought*? Excuse me, David, but I don't think you put a whole lot of thought into it."

"But I have a lot of things to button up before I go."

He actually thought he could dump her, and she'd still do his work? Rita stared at him with open-mouthed amazement, only coming out of her daze when she heard a tapping on the door. Sighing, she let Miss Pettybottham and Brody in. "Miss Caroline Pettybottham, this is David Parr, the new vice president of the Paris office."

Miss Pettybottham held out her hand, and when David pressed his lips to it, she asked, "Getting in practice for the French ladies?" Even after he let go of her hand, she still stood too close to his side.

He smiled. "No, *ma chère*, I hear the Texas gals are far more beautiful."

Rita grabbed his laptop from the table and shoved it into his chest, knocking him back. "Do your own report, Casanova!"

"He was Italian."

"And you're mud. Get out. Now."

"There are only a few minor additions to make. I'm sure you could do them in an hour or two."

Brody took a step forward, but Miss Pettybottham stopped him. "Are you going back to Boise this afternoon, Mr. Parr? Because it seems as though I've had automobile difficulties and I'm in dreadful need of a ride." She waved her fingers at the laptop. "I'm sure any additions or changes can wait—David."

He bowed slightly and smiled, then held out his arm. "I'd be happy to." As she followed the couple out of the house, Rita heard him ask, "May I call you 'Caroline'?"

David waved to Rita as he backed the SUV out of the driveway, and she stood on the porch until the car disappeared down the road. There went her carefully planned life. All her dreams. Everything she'd worked the last ten years for had almost…almost been hers.

Rita's shoulders sagged. Not just her personal life was in tatters. "There went the last chance for the children's home funding." Caroline Pettybottham had been in the house all of two minutes, and they hadn't even discussed the project.

Brody stepped behind her and gently massaged her neck. "Don't worry, we'll get along somehow."

While she was certain he was wrong—continuing operation

depended solely on Caroline Pettybottham's good graces—he was right on with the massage, connecting with every tense muscle in her neck. She could have sworn his fingers were magic. "And there went any future I had with Pettybottham Enterprises."

"I doubt it. Even the Pettybotthams couldn't be that petty—so to speak."

She sighed, knowing a cowboy just couldn't understand big business. So she changed the subject to another dreary topic. "I'm glad I didn't send out the invitations."

"Invitations?"

"To the wedding. They're all engraved and addressed, sitting on my desk at home in Seattle. What a waste of money."

"See if Pettybottham Enterprises will reimburse you."

"Hardly." Angry as she was, his gentle massage relaxed her and she leaned into him. His breath brushed her cheek and he folded his arms around her waist, clasping his hands on her tummy. Somehow, her troubles didn't seem so tormenting.

He turned her around to face him and held her face in his hands. "Rita Markum, I'm going to kiss you."

She gazed into his midnight blue eyes and nearly melted on the spot. She wouldn't say yes and she couldn't say no. It didn't matter, he didn't wait for an answer.

The first brush of his lips on hers sent fiery tingles swirling deep in her. He urged her mouth open and touched her tongue with his. Her knees nearly buckled.

"Rita, get me a pain pill, please," her mother called from her bedroom.

They sprang apart.

"Oh. Dear." She touched her lips. "Mom." Happy for a reason to escape him, she turned tail and escaped into her mother's bedroom, only to have to turn around and face the only man who'd ever made her lose all sensibility. "Uh, I forgot the pill."

He opened the cabinet and handed her the bottle. She fled

back to her mother's room.

"Water?" Judy asked.

Rita groaned. When she returned to the kitchen, he held out a tall glass of ice water. "Thanks."

After she gave the pill and the water to Judy, she sat in the bedside chair. "I have to tell you straight-out, Mom. David just broke our engagement."

Judy frowned, but didn't say anything.

"Uh, he took a position in Paris. He'd already made up his mind to go, with or without me. And of course I can't go, because I wouldn't have the chance for advancement that I would stateside, so. . ."

"So you don't love him and he came here to say his good-byes."

If only he'd been that decent, maybe she wouldn't have the roiling, bitter burning in her stomach every time she thought of him. Had he been using her the last three years they'd been dating? Then again, she'd been using him in a way, although certainly not to his detriment.

"He came here so I could work on his report."

"Doesn't sound very gentlemanly. Maybe it's best he's out of the picture. You're smart and you're beautiful, honey. It won't be long before another young buck will be courting you. Besides, I never did cotton to David's lack of manners to his elders."

"He was the best partner for me, Mom. I can't imagine who would be better, at least, not in the Seattle office." Rita slouched in the chair and put her foot up on the bed. I think I'll stay here for a while."

"Don't you have a guest waiting for you in the kitchen?"

Facing Brody after that bone-melting kiss held no allure. Every allure, actually. "Yes, Brody's out there."

Judy patted Rita's foot. "I know he's a cowboy—worse, actually—but he's our neighbor, and you'll just have to cowboy up and learn to get along with him for the next few weeks." She yawned. "Now, run along. These pills are kicking in."

Rita left the room, closing the door softly, then leaned against it and let out another deep sigh. Oh, she got along with Brody all right. Too darned well, in fact. She felt like dry kindling and he was a Diamond Strike-Anywhere Match.

He'd struck out. Brody cursed under his breath when Rita waltzed back into the kitchen cool as a bag of fish in Cow Creek, while he was hot as a horny toad in August.

Then again, he did need to cut her a little slack considering that her boyfriend had just broken up with her without missing a step. In truth, David had been downright heartless. Rita seemed to be holding up well, or maybe she was one of those people who had delayed reactions. At any rate, Brody didn't intend to remind Rita of her former fiancé if he could help it.

He ached for her. Every minute he was with her, he wanted her more.

Keeping himself in check, he tried to match her indifference. "I'd like you and Judy to join us at the rodeo in Jordan this weekend. I have extra tickets."

She shook her head. "That's a three-hour drive, at least. Mom isn't recovered enough for a trip like that." Rita turned on the faucet and squirted some dish soap into the sink. "We'll have to pass on this one."

"Sure? We could put her in my camper."

"With Socrates, I suppose."

"Naw, he doesn't like to ride in it for some reason. I'll be taking the horse trailer. Perseus and Guinevere can ride up front with us."

Turning around and cocking one hip against the sink, she said, "If anyone rides back there, it'll be me. I'm taking care of my mother."

The phone rang and he cursed again. He'd have to start all over with his cajoling now.

Rita answered it and after a pause said, "Mrs. Petty-bottham?" She looked into the handset, then putting it back to her ear, said, "*The* Mrs. Pettybottham?"

Too exasperated to even think, Brody clenched his fists, wishing he could hear the other end of the conversation, too. His mother was up to something sneaky, as usual. Somehow, he'd head her off because he could *not* let her use Rita as a pawn. Rita deserved better than that, and when he got home, he'd call his mother and give her the what-for. While he'd grown up amidst her plans and schemes, Rita was an innocent bystander and, by damn, he refused to let her get caught in the crossfire.

Rita pressed the end button and she stood there staring at the phone with a silly grin on her face. Then she let out a war-whoop and danced around the kitchen table.

Brody hooked his thumbs in his belt. "Well?"

"Well, I've just been offered the position of Vice President of International Operations for Pettybottham Enterprises." She smiled smugly. "I'm now David's boss. Revenge! Bwaha-haha."

Brody laughed. "I take it your broken heart has healed."

She shrugged. "I'll be moving to Houston."

"When?"

"End of the year. Mrs. Pettybottham didn't want me to shortchange my mom, *and* I don't have to use my vacation time. She's giving me an extra month here, two if needed, and another month to tie up ends at the Seattle office. What a sweet woman."

He'd heard his mother called a lot of things, but never a sweet woman. Justifiably so. In no time, Rita would learn that the acting CEO of Pettybottham Enterprises could out-maneuver the keenest minds in business, and sweetness had never been one of her tactics. Ever. "That's nice. Congratulations."

As Rita danced another little jig around the table, she scooped up the dirty cups and tossed them in the dishwater. "Oh, Brody, this is a dream job!" Then she tilted her head, frowning pensively. "But how did she even know I'm alive?"

Because he'd told her—that may have been the biggest mistake of his life. And hers. "Good employers know who their best people are."

"She's ordering my letterhead and business cards today, and wants me to order furniture for my office. This is a new position at Pettybottham." Her eyes sparkled, not unlike they had after their kiss. "Isn't this a stroke of good luck?"

He wasn't so sure.

The next morning, Rita helped Judy into the kitchen chair and asked to see the grocery list. "I might want to add a few things."

"Chocolate?" Judy's sparkling eyes matched her jubilant smile.

"Of course. Gotta have the primary food group." She chewed on her pencil as she looked over her mom's two pages of grocery and supplies items. "That's a lot to ask Brody to pick up." Then she saw the personal items. "You can't possibly ask him to buy some of this stuff."

"I figured on you going with him," Judy said.

"Really, Mom—" Rita glanced sideways at her mother. "You shouldn't be left alone. It's too soon after your surgery." That's all she needed—to buy sanitary napkins with Brody standing next to her.

"Nonsense, I'll be fine. You've hovered over me like a mother hen and I need a little alone time." She patted her latest Leigh Greenwood western romance. "And I have a book to read."

"What if you need to lie down?"

"Luke's just a phone call away."

"That's what I'm afraid of."

Her mom just laughed. "I'm fifty-two years old and I don't need a chaperone."

"Hrmph." For all her admonitions about avoiding cowboys, Judy Markum wasn't exactly walking the talk. On the other hand, she'd been widowed for many years, and maybe she deserved a man to grow old with her.

But a busted-up cowboy—how long would he live? Would Judy spend ten years of her life nursing him just like she had her husband? "Just how serious are you about Luke?"

With a shrug, Judy opened her book. "Depends on how serious he is about me. He's been pretty cagey." She put the book down and looked up. "Rita, honey, it's time we had a talk."

Rita didn't like the sound of this at all.

"Luke and I have known each other for thirty-some years. I met him at a Little Britches Rodeo—he rode steers and I ran the barrels. We dated. In fact, we were engaged."

Although shocked, Rita put on her poker face. "That was before you met Dad, then?"

"Yes."

"So why did you break up?"

"Because he went on the circuit and I was all alone. I met your dad—he had to forego the season because of a broken leg. I was lonesome, we got married, and you were born."

Rita thought there seemed to be a lot missing in the story. "Six months later."

"The first one can come anytime. After that, your father started rodeoing again." She whisked her fingers. "Now, go on. Brody has to get back to his place in time to load his show gear before dark. Leave Beauty here with me."

As Rita was walking out, her mom called, "Oh, and we're going to Jordan Valley with Luke and him tomorrow."

Biting her lip, Rita folded the shopping list and stuffed it in her Levi's pocket. She'd save that battle for later.

"This is my lucky day." Brody opened the passenger door for Rita, who scowled at him before she climbed into the rig. Beauty stared at him in her forlorn half-bloodhound way. "No, Judy needs you home this time, Beauty. You'll have to stay."

After he'd taken his place in the driver's seat, Rita said,

"You won't think you're so lucky when you find out what all Mom needs." She held up a two-page list. "Besides groceries and dry goods, we need some grain and hay, plus a few veterinarian supplies."

"I might as well take the horse trailer, then, since we're low on grain, too, and Perseus could use a couple fifty-pound bags of dog food."

At his place, he hitched up the trailer with Perseus, Guinevere, and Socrates all giving him the sad-eye. "Ah, what the heck." He opened the trailer gate. "Get in, but you have to promise to behave yourselves in town."

Socrates brayed at Brody as he shut the gate.

As he passed the window, he shook his finger at the mule. "I mean it. You stay where I put you this time." He let the dog and skunk into the backseat and finally settled behind the wheel.

"Another day, another menagerie," Rita murmured.

"They're like kids," he explained. "Every once in a while you have to take them places so they remember their manners."

He couldn't resist glancing at the little strip of skin that showed between her white T-shirt and her jeans. She filled out the T-shirt rather well, as a matter of fact. With a little luck, it would rain. He'd love to see her in the rain.

Down the road a ways, he checked to see if his cell phone was still roaming. It was. He'd been trying to reach his mother since she'd called Rita, but either she was nowhere to be found, or she was avoiding his call. Sometimes Caller ID irked him.

While he'd rather get buckshot in the eye than go shopping, the pretty woman sitting beside him at least made for damned good scenery, if not good conversation. The drive from Grasmere to Melba didn't offer a whole lot besides scrub sagebrush and alkali, and the road from Melba to Nampa was nicer, but the atmosphere in the cab was just as tense.

"Have you given any more thought about going to the rodeo with us?" He turned the air conditioner up full-tilt.

"No, but Mom has. She says we're going, but I told her that

she shouldn't."

He took a long draw of water from the canteen and offered it to Rita. "She'll be fine. Many a laid-up cowboy has lain in that bed while I carted him to the next show. In fact, I've had to do that myself a time or two. I have two custom beds back there, comfortable as can be. And if she gets tired during the rodeo, we can take her there to rest."

The set of her lips and slight frown caused him to wonder what he'd said wrong.

Several minutes passed. She took a few sips and shoved the cork in. "Is Luke going?"

He tried to decide if Luke's presence would be a plus or a minus. Didn't matter, though. "Yup. He hasn't been to a rodeo all summer, so I hired the neighbor boy to feed the stock—and your mom's."

"So you think you have all the bases covered, then."

"Yup."

They discussed the stores they needed to go to and planned their route. Other than that, the silence of the two-hour drive was broken only by Perseus' occasional yip at a rabbit, or Guinevere's squeak when the dog stepped on her tail.

In the feedstore, Rita stood beside Brody as he signed the credit card slip, tapped his knuckles on the counter and headed for the door.

"You settle up your part of the bill and go to Albertson's while I get this feed loaded," he said as he left.

After paying the clerk for her mom's purchases, Rita hurried after him. "I'll help you, then we'll go to the store together."

"Nope, it'll be a whole lot faster if you can buy the groceries while I load the trailer. I'll meet you at Albertson's in an hour."

"Oh, for Pete's sake!" Rita eyed the most exasperating man she'd ever met. "You can't load fifty-pound bags of feed with a broken arm."

"You can either watch, or you can buy groceries." He hefted a bag into the horse trailer and pushed it to the front.

Remembering the certain items on her grocery list, she opted to let him ruin himself. "Suit yourself. You could hire a boy to stack those bags for five bucks. I'm sure some teenager around here could use the money, too."

"I can load up before I could find a kid to do it." He wiped the sweat from his brow with his forearm. "See you in an hour."

The mule stood beside the trailer, ears cocked.

"You're against me, too, aren't you, Socrates?" Blowing out her frustration, she set out on a brisk walk to the grocery store three blocks way. Living two hours from civilization, shopping took on a different character than when she lived in her Seattle condo with a grocery store across the street. Her mom simply couldn't run to the store for a can of tomato paste, so she had to buy several months' worth of supplies at a time, especially with winter coming.

An hour later, she pushed the last of four fully-packed carts to the checkout line and hoped the cashier would get everything bagged before Brody showed up. But sure enough, the minute the clerk scanned the sanitary napkins, Guess-Who materialized at her side.

The clerk hit the total button and Rita swiped her card, wishing the box girl would bag the offending items, but she wandered off to help a little old lady. Nothing like being abandoned in the time of need.

A blood-curdling scream and a siren saved the day. Not that she wished ill will toward anyone, but at least it got Brody out the door. Two box boys came to her rescue while she signed the charge slip. Pushing one cart, she led the way into the parking lot while one box boy pushed the second cart and pulled the third, and the other teenager pushed the fourth.

Halfway to the pickup, she saw Brody sprint across the street to an Animal Control truck. She checked the cab—no Perseus. No Guinevere! She hastily unlocked the camper and peered in, but they weren't there, either.

"Would you load these for me?" she asked the young men,

who'd both be lookers once they grew into their ears and feet.

"Sure."

Flipping them each a five, she dodged cars as she ran across the street. Brody argued with the officer while a dejected Guinevere sat in a small cage in the back of the officer's truck. Her tail drooped, and she held a long-stemmed red rose in her teeth.

Rita leaned into the truck, within a foot of the cage. "Don't worry, Guinny. Brody will get you out of jail as soon as he can."

"Rita, get her rabies certificate out of the glove box." Turning back to the Animal Control officer, he said, "I have a show tomorrow in Jordan. She didn't scratch or bite anyone, her papers are in order, so please just let me pay the fine and take her home."

Fetching the papers as fast as she could, she dashed back and handed them to Brody, her heart racing not so much from the run as from the dread of telling him that Perseus was also missing. That could wait.

The officer looked at the certificate, then filled out the form on his ticket book. "I'll let it go this time, but keep your animal caged. Mail fifty dollars to the courthouse." He ripped off the ticket and gave it to Brody. "I don't want to see your dang skunk in this town again."

"Thank you, sir." Brody stuffed the ticket into his shirt pocket. "I think Guinevere has all of Nampa she wants for a while." He retrieved the skunk from the cage. "C'mon, Rita. Let's get out of here. Two hundred for flowers and a fifty-dollar ticket is all I need for one day."

Scarcely able to keep up with him, she tapped him on the arm. "Uh, Brody?"

"Yeah."

"Perseus isn't in the cab."

"Did you look in the trailer? If Guinevere got out, more than likely Perseus did, too. He likes to ride with Socrates, but I won't let him because I'm afraid he'll get stepped on."

As they approached the pickup, Rita heard frantic barking and lots of hollering coming from Albertson's. Perseus bounded toward them full tilt and tail wagging. Covered from nose to ears with icing, he dropped a bride and groom figurine partially covered with white icing at Brody's feet. She could have sworn that the dog cocked his head at her and smiled, the icing weighing down his whiskers.

Brody, on the other hand, wasn't smiling at all. "Get the animals in the cab." He tipped up the brim of his hat and rubbed his temple. "Looks like I better go in and pay for someone's wedding cake."

She opened the door and put the skunk on the seat. She grabbed a towel from the floorboard and wiped the dog's face and paws before she let him in. "I hope you didn't ruin someone's marriage ceremony," she murmured, thinking about the seven-tier cake she'd picked out for her and David's reception. It would have been beautiful. But wrong—the wedding, that is. She knew that now—had maybe known it all along. Still, a tear welled up for dreams that could've been. Should have been.

Hopefully, Brody could make it right with the store and the couple, but he'd spent a lot of money today, and multi-tiered cakes were neither cheap nor quick to make.

"And you know," she said to the animals, "it's upsetting to even think about those beautifully engraved invitations I have to throw in the garbage."

Guinevere jumped on her lap and Rita patted her on the head. "Who'd have thought that instead of finalizing my house design, I'd be sitting in a pickup in Idaho, of all places, petting a skunk." The skunk rubbed her jaw on Rita's arm.

David had shown his stripes, and she far preferred to see them now than see them later. The frustrating part was why she hadn't recognized his true character before.

Brody got into the pickup and jammed the keys into the ignition. "A hundred and fifty bucks," he said as he started the engine. "And they wouldn't even take any money for the labor of cleaning up the mess. I offered, but the manager said it was part of doing business. She said they had plenty of time to make another one."

He turned his gaze to her and her insides turned to jelly. Against her better judgment, she reached for his arm, but he caught her hand and kissed each fingertip. The tingles shot through her arm down her torso, and settled down deep. She squirmed in the seat to get comfortable.

Trying to hold her voice steady, she said, "You've had a rotten day. I'm so sorry." She pulled her hand away from his, but the memory of his lips on her fingers remained.

He shifted into first gear. "Let's go." His husky voice reverberated through her.

After she relaxed her throat, she glanced at him. "Uh, I need a rest stop before we go back home. Two hours can be a very long time."

"Me, too, come to think of it. Might as well fuel up and get water for Socrates while we're at it." He pointed across the street. "I'll go to that Shell station over there."

At the pump, Brody took the fueling and window washing duty while Rita went to the restroom, then to the store to buy some chips, pop, and doggie treats. As she paid, she heard Brody curse vehemently. Grabbing the purchases, she hightailed out to the trailer, where he stood scowling.

No Socrates. Hesitant to spark his anger any further, she waited for him to quit gritting his teeth and say something.

He slammed the gate. "You'd think he'd leave a danged note or something."

The tic in his jaw and the set of his lips indicated she should keep her amusement to herself, but she couldn't stop herself. "Maybe he didn't have a pencil and paper."

"Get in. I'll drive back to the Alberson's lot and park. You take one side of the street, and I'll take the other. We'll meet at the feed store. Make good and sure Perseus and Guinevere stay in the pickup."

"Okay."

"I never could keep that dang mule penned up if he didn't want to be. He was in the trailer when I drove to the grocery store, though. He must have left while we were gathering up the other two animals."

They didn't search for long. A police car with a flashing light led them to a jewelry store where a short, bald man's eyes bulged as he hollered and waved his arms. "Get that beast out of my store!"

People stood around, chuckling, adding to the redness of his face, clear to the top of his shiny dome. The officers stood at the door, peering in. "You get him. I'll call Animal Control," one said.

"No, I have seniority. *You* get him. I'll work the radio."

"Mules kick."

"So do captains."

Brody tapped the senior officer on the shoulder. "He's mine. I'll get him."

Both officers stepped back, allowing Brody and Rita to enter. The glass of one display case had been broken.

After looking around to assess the damage, Brody turned to the officers. "Ask the owner how much this case will cost me."

Nodding at the mule, the older officer replied, "I think he'll want your mule out of his shop, first."

"Oh. Yeah." Brody turned to Socrates and patted him on the rump. "You and I are going to have a nice little conversation later. For now, you go back to the trailer with Rita."

Socrates tossed his head.

"Goldang," the younger man said. "I think he said, 'yes.'"

Rita held Socrates' halter while he calmly ambled out of the store seemingly unfazed by all the hullabaloo surrounding him. As she opened the gate of the trailer, he turned to her and nuzzled her hand. She felt something drop into her palm. A wedding ring set.

"Oh, Socrates, Brody's not going to like this." She patted

the mule on the withers. "Get in and wait for us. I need to take this back to the jeweler before they put us all in jail and throw away the key."

He hopped into the trailer and Rita secured the latch and hoped he'd stay put for once. She wondered how Brody tolerated such an obnoxious beast—although he did have a certain charm. The mule, that is.

She dodged the cars as she ran back to the store, where Brody waited patiently for the owner to stop ranting and raving. When the man finally shut up long enough to wipe the sweat from his head with his sleeve, Brody asked, "How much?"

"Five hundred dollars."

"For one little piece of glass?"

"It had an alarm in it. Five hundred dollars. Plus a hundred for installation, and another five hundred for lost business."

With a glance at the officer, Brody reached for the wallet in his hip pocket. Rita tapped his arm and when he leaned toward her, she held out the mule-slobbered wedding ring set. He froze, then gazed at her questioningly. She nodded. "He gave it to me when I trailered him," she whispered.

"Why'd he have to pick the one with a rock the size of Rhode Island?" He took the ring and wiped it on his shirt, then handed it to the owner, who backed away and refused to take it.

"The ring's damaged."

"You didn't even look at it!"

"No bride is going to want a ring that has been in a mule's mouth."

When both officers crossed their arms over their chests, Rita didn't think Brody had a chance to win this round, either.

Apparently, neither did he. "How much?"

"Eight thousand plus tax."

Handing the owner his VISA, he mumbled, "I'm gonna wring that mule's neck."

After the transaction was complete, Brody took Rita's arm. "Let's get out of here."

"Mister," the owner called. "You forgot your wedding set."

Brody snatched it off the cracked case and shoved it in his shirt pocket.

She could hardly believe that a rodeo clown would have such a high limit on his credit card, but apparently he did. Something about him just didn't wash.

Chapter 8

You'd think Brody would be more appreciative of my efforts, but come to think of it, I don't think he ever got the hint. We mules must have the patience of Job while we wait for our humans to recognize the truth.

Anyone can tell that Brody could hardly keep his hands off Rita, and that she's equally struck by him. Why they keep themselves in such firm isolation is beyond me. I have to remind myself how stubborn humans can be. And dense. They're both goodhearted people and they both consider themselves honest, but both of them are lying to themselves and we mules consider that the most dishonest thing one can do.

But they aren't mules. If they were, we wouldn't have to go to all this trouble.

Perseus failed to get the wedding cake. Apparently it fell on top of him while he was dragging it off the table. He did manage to save the little statue of the bride and groom, though, so I'm sure we can put that to use. And Guinevere did swipe one red rose, although she said she had to suffer untold indignities to her skunkness to get it. While I was hoping she'd manage to get a bouquet, there's something quite elegant about a single, long-stemmed red rose. I'm hoping it doesn't wilt before we can put it to use. For now, Rita has it in a Coke bottle full of water. I noticed that she breathes in the fragrance every once in a while, so maybe there's hope for her yet.

As for the wedding ring, naturally I scored one there. The prettiest one in the store, although I'd have preferred a larger stone, is safe and sound in my human's pocket. I'm sure it will look beautiful on Rita's long, slender finger. All I have to do is get Brody to put it there.

One success—Beauty reports that Luke spent the whole day with Judy and she seems to welcome his company. While Luke isn't our primary objective, he is companionable, at least for a human, and we'd all like to see him find a mate. Beauty, of course, is more concerned about Judy wasting her time on false notions while holding the love of her life at leg's length.

Another opportunity is coming up tomorrow and we plan to take full advantage of it. I haven't devised a plan, yet, but I'll have one in place before we reach Jordan Valley. All we need to do is get that ring on Rita's finger, and I'll be happy to stay in the corral and munch on hay. Part of the time, anyway.

"Stop!"

Brody stepped on the brakes. Rita sounded distressed, but he didn't want to throw Socrates head-over-tea kettle, even if the ornery mule did deserve it. "What's the matter?"

"Back up." She stuck her head out the window and looked down the road. "I saw something."

Relieved that she was all right, he turned the wheel. "I'll pull over. Backing a trailer up a hill at dusk isn't my idea of a good time."

"Oh, right." She jumped out of the pickup before it came to a complete stop and took off at a dead run. By the time he caught up with her, she was hunkered over a dead porcupine.

"You wanted me to stop for road-kill?"

"No, I wanted you to stop for a baby. A female porcupine would have babies now, so I had to check." She took a stick and gently pushed a little gray-brown pincushion away from its mother's lifeless body. "His mama was killed, but he's okay." She wrinkled her brow in a nurturing way. "He's not even weaned yet." Gingerly, she scooted it onto her hand and looked up. "See? His quills haven't even hardened."

Her jeans, white tank top, her hair pulled back into a ponytail—what a beautiful picture she created as she knelt beside the baby beast. She looked more like a country girl every day, and acted like one, too. "Rita, what are you going to do with a dang porcupine?" He helped her to her feet and brushed the dust off her knees, wishing there'd been dirt on that nice derriere of hers.

She shrugged, her indifferent gesture belying the mother-bear look on her face. "What do you do with a skunk?"

"That's different. Guinny's a show animal."

Rita set her jaw and glared at him. "Whatever. I'm taking care of this little guy for now and then we can figure out what to do with him. I guess it all depends on whether he can make it in the wild on his own."

Brody conceded, secretly glad that she'd insisted. "I guess it's the right thing to do. We can't leave him here to die."

Her wide grin was his reward. A man couldn't help but cave in to a woman like her.

"C'mon. I'll find a box to put him in." Not only did she heat up his blood, he thought as he headed for the pickup, she showed extraordinary kindness to animals. Even his obnoxious menagerie. The wedding ring seemed to tingle in his shirt pocket.

When he got back to the pickup, he scrounged in the bags of groceries until he found a box of microwave popcorn. With his pocketknife, he sliced the perimeter of one broad side, removed the packets of popcorn, and lined the box with his handkerchief.

"Here you go, porcupine nursery." He handed her the box. "Blue, even."

"Thanks." Her glowing smile warmed him right down to his. . .he'd better not think about that. She placed the baby in the middle of the popcorn box and gently scrunched the cloth all around to keep the tiny animal warm. "On closer inspection, I found that we'll need to change to pink."

"I'm fresh out of pink handkerchiefs."

"Odds are, you've never owned one."

"Your odds are correct."

"And in honor of my new job, I'm naming this little cutey Mrs. Pretty Bottom."

Brody chuckled at the thought of how his mother would take such a dubious honor.

Ah, Rita. So beautiful, so smart, and so. . .not his. Yet.

Brody and Rita drove another hour before they passed Grasmere and turned off on the road to their respective ranches. The day had been stressful and Rita couldn't have been happier to be home. Sitting in the pickup for four hours next to a man who had a double dose of testosterone and a triple dose of charm had taken its toll. Luckily, she had the animals to divert her attention. Mrs. Pretty Bottom was way too lethargic to be healthy and Rita hoped the tiny porcupine would respond once she had something to eat.

He stopped at the mailboxes and Rita retrieved their mail. Luke came out to meet them as they drove up to her mom's house. "Have a good day?"

Rita and Brody groaned in unison.

Luke shook his head and hid a grin with the brim of his hat. "I'll unload Judy's stuff," he said to Rita. "You go on inside and keep her company."

Glad to escape Brody's nearness, she gathered the mail and the box with the baby porcupine. "Thanks."

In her mom's bedroom, she handed Judy the letter from MOMMI. "You open this. After the fool I made of myself, I'm scared to."

"Don't know why. We've already been rejected. How bad can it get?" She ripped the side of the envelope and pulled out the letter. A check fluttered to her lap.

Rita snatched it and stared at the number. "Holy smoke. This is more than triple the amount I applied for." Clutching it to her chest, she jumped around the room, squealing like a schoolgirl, no dignity whatsoever, then bent over the bed and hugged the stuffin' out of her mother.

Judy waved the letter and grinned. "Says here she reconsidered and appreciates the efforts of those who take care of their own." Judy picked up the phone and punched a number. "Wait'll I tell Phyllis!" She pointed her thumb at the door. "You go tell Luke and Brody."

"First, I have a present for you. You have to feed it." She dashed into the kitchen, heated some milk and took it along with the porcupine and an eyedropper to her mom. "We found this little gal beside the road."

"Oh, how cute!" Judy filled the dropper and urged the baby's mouth open. "She's a little listless, though. Could be too late."

"I'm hoping your TLC will change that, Mom."

"Me, too." Judy cocked her head toward the door. "Now, git! Go tell the men about the check." She giggled. "I just can't believe our good fortune. Hopefully, this baby porcupine will have the same luck."

Rita skipped outside with the check, looking for Brody. She found him in the barn dumping a sack of chicken feed into the grain bin. She ran to him and flung her arms around his waist before she realized what she'd done.

He caught her and held her tight, brushing a kiss across her cheek. Her knees weak, she clung to him and kissed him on the mouth. He responded instantly with his tongue. And lower.

"I'll take it," he murmured.

"Take what?"

"Whatever you offer."

Realizing what she'd done, she pushed back, flushed and breathless, and showed him the check. "We have funding! I thought I'd blown it completely, but for some reason, MOMMI funded the building materials and at least three years of operational costs."

He flashed her a genuine smile and her heart melted. "This weekend is my last rodeo of the season, so I'll get a work party together next week and we'll get that house built."

She wanted to hug him again, but thought better of it. She'd fought her reactions to him all she could for one day, and after all that, nearly slipped and let him do what she desperately wanted him to do. The worst part was, Brody Alexander was truly a kind man. Too bad he engaged in one of the most hazardous professions ever invented by mankind.

While her future children wouldn't have a grandfather, she'd see to it that they had a father—one in good health.

The wisps of blonde hair brushing her pink-tinged cheeks nearly undid Brody, but the happiness in her eyes as she held up the check was worth all his frustration. He wished he'd told Caroline to send twice as much.

"We'll put most of this in CD's," she said. "We might as well be earning interest on the excess."

"Leave it to you to think of that." He tweaked her cheek. "The children around here are lucky to have you."

She smiled, her eyes passionately dark. "And you. They adore you."

"I'm flashy, but you, Judy, and Phyllis each give them something more important. Your business sense will keep the children's home in good shape."

"Naw, crunching numbers is the easy part, no sacrifice at all. Mom and Phyllis have the tough jobs. I won't even be here most of the time."

He inched toward her, backing her against a stall. "Rita Markum," he murmured in her ear, "I have never met a woman like you." He ran his hands over her sides and brushed her breasts, then lowered his head and kissed her as gently as he could, resisting the urge to throw her over his shoulder and haul her to the straw pile.

She kneaded the muscles in his back, pulling him closer. Glad to oblige, he deepened the kiss, tasting her, breathing in her lilac scent. When the kiss ended, she breathed out, then gently pushed on his chest. Reluctantly, he stepped back.

"I have to go back in the house." Her voice sounded breathless and her cheeks were flushed. "Mom's calling Phyllis and I need to get the groceries put away in case she comes over." Her words came a little too fast, so he reckoned their kiss had rattled her as much as it had him. "There isn't a single place in the whole kitchen to sit. It'll take me an hour to straighten up."

"Shhhh," he said, moving toward her, drowning in her blue eyes. "One more kiss, then you can go."

Her mouth opened slightly and she licked her lower lip, sending all the blood from his brain south. He flicked his tongue where hers had been, then closed in for another deep, slow kiss. "Come with me, Rita."

"No," she whispered, her eyes contradicting her. "I can't. Not you."

She broke away and ran into the house, clutching the check to her breast. He'd have given everything he had to be where that check was. Why she seemed to be afraid to get close to him, he couldn't venture to guess, but parts of him were growing more and more frustrated. She didn't seem to be the snobbish type, who would look down on a man she didn't think was her equal either socially or economically, so that wasn't it. And she was attracted to him as much as he was to her, of that he had no doubt.

"Damn!" He flung his Stetson across the barn and it landed on a bale of hay.

Unloading the rest of the feed proved a godsend. Nothing like good, hard physical exercise to work off excessive passion. He wondered again what she had against him. It couldn't be their confrontation all those years ago—not after the kisses they'd shared. No, she had some other reason, and he planned to find out what it was.

No, he wouldn't. A wife and kids would never tolerate his life on the rodeo circuit. Frowning, he tossed another bag of grain on the pile. A wife and kids? He gulped. The very thought scared him half to death. All he wanted was a good time.

The wedding ring in his shirt pocket rested heavily against his chest. He outlined the circle with his fingertip, then grabbed another fifty-pound bag of cattle feed. The ring had to go. He'd put it in the safe first thing when he got home.

"We're staying for supper," Luke said as he stepped over the threshold and ducked through the door. "Judy has a nice meal waiting for us in the oven."

"Rita's gonna be madder than a wet hen when she finds out Judy has been on her feet and cooking." Brody put down the bag of feed and sat on it. "You make any headway today?"

"Naw, I'm takin' it slow." Luke grabbed a pitchfork and rested it on his shoulder. "She's made it clear for many years that she don't want no busted-up cowboy, but I think she does."

"You two make a nice couple, and she seems to be softening up some."

"Looks like it. Might pop the question this weekend. Keep Rita busy, will you?"

"My pleasure." Brody couldn't think of anything he'd rather do than keep Rita *busy*. "Does Judy know there aren't any rooms left at the hotel and that all four of us will be sharing the camper?"

"She knows. She said not to mention that to her daughter."

Brody nodded, then stood and tossed the sack of grain he'd been sitting on into the storeroom, trying not to think about sleeping within three feet of Rita for two nights. He hoped he could endure it. Talk about sweet torture.

An hour later, supper with the Markum ladies was full of teasing and easy camaraderie on the surface, but buzzed with an undercurrent of desire and need as they passed the biscuits and gravy. Certainly, Brodie had need—it came in handy as a napkin hook.

Luke forked a fist-sized hunk of roast beef onto his plate. "So you're a grandmother to a porcupine now?"

Judy giggled, and Rita smirked. Brody wondered what was going through that mathematical head of hers. She seemed to like Luke, even had kidded around with him, but her frustration at his familiarity with her mother shined through every once in a while with an uplifted brow and a deep sigh.

"Yes, Rita never could let nature take its course. Long as I've had her, I've had animals to feed."

"Mom, I wasn't that bad."

"Ground squirrels, horned toads, not to mention half-starved cats and dogs." Judy shook her head as she reminisced. "No snakes, though. I can't abide any form of snake, no matter whether they eat mice or not."

"No, she made me keep those in the doghouse. We didn't have Beauty yet, and Old Cassias had already died."

"I wasn't too happy when she couldn't find them the next day."

"Nope, we never did find them. Then Mr. Johnson—he owned your place then—told me that snakes hibernate when it's cold, so I left them alone after that."

Luke and Brody ate while the ladies talked. After Luke finished, he leaned back and rested his hand on the back of Judy's chair. The gesture didn't escape Rita's notice. She frowned, then did her best to ignore them. To distract her, Brody put his hand on her chair, too.

He liked sitting in the kitchen with a smart, beautiful woman with more fire than Mt. St. Helens. Certainly, anyone could tell that Luke doted on Judy, and Brody hoped the lady would consent to be Luke's wife. They'd both lost their spouses and deserved a chance to be happy together.

When the two men got home, Brody had his own little surprise in the mail from his sister. "Ah, heck."

"You have a problem?" Luke asked as he hung his hat on the nail by the door.

"You could say that." Except he couldn't even tell Luke about it. His foreman had no idea what kind of money his boss had, or that in college, Brody had been named the Most Eligible Bachelor of the Year by *Ladies' World Magazine* after they'd dogged him for months to get photos. At least, Broderick

Alexander Pettybottham the Fourth had been—the long-haired jetsetter with the largest Prada sunglasses on the market.

Brody didn't think anyone would connect him with the Most Eligible Bachelor of the Year, especially Luke, who had never touched a woman's magazine in his life. Brody swore to do his level damnedest to make sure Luke wouldn't ever find out.

Brody crumpled his sister's letter of resignation and tossed it in the garbage. MOMMI no longer had a director. *Rita could do it!* No, she'd find out about him in a heartbeat. She'd be danged good, though. Heck, he could even move the MOMMI headquarters to Grasmere. But no, he told himself again, it would never work. He needed someone who knew his true identity, but didn't mind that he lived to fight bulls. If Rita knew who he really was, she'd be stiff competition with his mother for conniving to get him back into the corporate fold.

Later, after Luke went out to finish up the chores, Brody finally got his mother on the phone.

"What's this about you creating a whole new position for Rita Markum?"

"Why, dear, I thought you'd be happy about that. You told me to promote her, and with half a dozen foreign offices, the workload was simply overwhelming. Your Miss Markum fills the bill quite nicely. She has an excellent work record and,"— Brody could just see her cat-eat-the canary-grin—"she has a superb reference."

Brody knew his mother wanted to keep an eye on Rita. Maybe she thought he was in love. Whatever her plan, it wouldn't work because even if he were in love, which he wasn't, and did have the notion to get married, which he didn't, Rita would never agree. "Just don't mess with her head. She's a nice lady—she doesn't need your interference."

"Have you heard from your sister?"

"Yes, I saw her yesterday, and I got an overnight letter from her today. She must have mailed it the minute she got to Boise."

"She's on her way to France."

"France?" Brody remembered David, who took Caroline to the airport. "For business?"

"No, she says she's found a new boy-toy."

"David Parr?"

"That's the one. Says she might stay for a year unless he gets boring." He heard his mother sigh. "I wish she'd quit that nonsense and find some nice man to marry. And anyway, there are some things a mother just doesn't want to know."

He doubted that. "She resigned as director of MOMMI."

"I know. What are you going to do?"

He shrugged. "I'll think of something."

"I'm sure you will."

But he knew she hoped he didn't. Whoever ran MOMMI would learn his secret, and he had to be very careful with his choice. "I've gotta go, Mother. Treat Miss Markum with respect."

So much for Rita's perfect fiancé. Sure, they'd broken up, but Brody knew she'd be hurt if she knew that Caroline had moved in already. He thought his sister had more sense than that. With her money and looks, she could get a good man. At least she could've waited a week.

Early the next morning, and over Rita's objections, she, her mom, and Mrs. Pretty Bottom rode to Jordan Valley with Brody and Luke. Guinevere, Perseus, and Beauty hadn't seemed at all happy to be relegated to the trailer with Socrates.

Despite Rita's maneuvering, she ended up in the front seat with Brody driving, and her mom sat in the backseat looking quite cozy with Luke. Rita decided not to rock the boat. Her mom deserved all the happiness in the world, and if she thought Luke could give it to her, then Rita would support that decision and welcome him into the family.

That decision, however, in no way nullified her own decision to stay away from a man who could very well live a short life with a painful and crippled end. As Brody was sure to do. Odds were high that his fearlessness and audacity in front of two-thousand-pound bulls would catch up with him eventually. She didn't plan to be around when that happened.

Brody turned off Highway 51 to the Owyhee Uplands Backcountry Byway.

"I didn't even know about this road."

He glanced at her and her insides went all firecrackery. "Beats going clear to Marsing and cutting over to 95 there. Hey, you wanna go to the dance after the Saturday show?"

She had to stop that tingly achiness that ping-ponged around her belly every time she caught his gaze or touched him. Or sat too near, like now. "If Mom goes, I'll go, although we can't let her over tire herself." She wetted her lips and studied the rolling hills and sagebrush as if she'd seen something interesting. What did interest her, she couldn't look at, lest he think she was interested. Which, of course, she wasn't.

A few hours later, and none too soon for her, they pulled into the rodeo grounds at Jordan Valley.

"This rodeo is a little, last-minute affair featuring only local cowboys," he said as he set the brake.

"Yes, Mom told me. I'll bet it'll be good, though." It had one of the best bullfighters she'd ever seen, for one thing. "It'll be the first rodeo I've been to since high school."

She tumbled out of the pickup and stretched her legs while Luke took out her mom's crutches, then carefully lifted her out, propping her up against him. Judy held onto his waist even after he'd offered her the crutches. Rita gritted a smile at them and hoped they'd both understand they had her blessing. After all, their relationship clearly was past the point of no return. Her effort was all for naught, however, because neither of them knew she existed at the moment. She wanted her mom to be happy, and she conceded that Luke was in pretty good health for an old bullrider, so he'd be around a few more years to take care of her mom, maybe into old age.

Brody brushed his arm across her back as he passed and

took her hand. "Come with me. I have to take care of the animals."

His magnetism would've forced her to follow him even if he hadn't grabbed her. She needed to keep her reactions to him in check a whole lot better.

He opened the camper door and dodged when Perseus bounded out. "Stay," he told the dog. "I'll take you for a walk as soon as I take care of the others."

Perseus whined, but immediately hunkered down, panting rapidly with his eyes alert, waiting his turn.

"I'll, uh, get Socrates," Rita murmured, seeing the opportunity to make her escape.

"Okay. I'll be with you in a minute."

"Never thought I'd be feedin' a gol-dern porkypine," she heard Luke grumble. Rita smiled. Yes, perhaps she really did need to reassess her thoughts. Any man who'd feed a baby porcupine with an eyedropper couldn't be all that bad a choice for a step-father.

She unlatched the gate and the miniature mule stepped out holding a brush in his teeth. With a giggle, she said, "Sure, Socrates, I'd be happy to groom you." She tied his lead rope to the latch and took the brush from his mouth. The mule leaned into her with every stroke, so she decided to give his withers and rump a little massaging, too. "Are you ready for tonight's show?"

He cocked his head and blinked, then tossed his head.

"What a talented mule you are. Brody's lucky to have you." She brushed his sparse mane. "How about we braid it and make you even more gorgeous?"

He nibbled gently on her pantleg.

Brody rounded the corner, grinned, and patted Socrates on the rump. "Hey there, old boy, are you making time with my girl?"

Warmth flooded her cheeks and her mouth went dry as their gazes met. If Brody Alexander worked at Pettybottham Enterprises, or anywhere but in front of a bull, she would've loved to be his girl. "You must admit, he's quite charming."

"And picks good rings, too."

Socrates tossed his head. *Pbbbbt!*

Rubbing the mule's ears, Brody said to Rita, "We have three hours before the show. If you don't mind finishing up with Socrates, I'll bathe Perseus and Guinny. That'll give me an hour to check my equipment and put on my greasepaint."

"Sure. Do you have any clear fingernail polish?"

Brody pointed to a huge fishing tackle box. "In there, with my greasepaint. You'll find rubber bands and some ornaments for his mane and tail in there, too. Use whatever you like, as long as Socrates approves."

Rita opened the box and found both clear and black polish. "Do you have a hoof block?" As she looked around she saw a block behind the box and put it under her arm. "Never mind." She cupped Socrates' chin in her hands. "We'll get those hooves polished up. What a flashy mule you'll be tonight."

She'd forgotten how serene she'd always felt grooming animals. In Seattle, she had never had any pets, not even a guppy. With her work schedule, she didn't have time to pay proper attention to one.

As she finished polishing his right front hoof, Brody brought a tub of water and the skunk. She sent him her best scowl. "Back away, buster!" She blew gently on the polish to help it dry and then faced him. "I don't want you messing up this fine pedicure."

He chuckled and moved the tub a few feet away. "Actually, Guinny enjoys her bath immensely. It's the dog you have to watch. Afterwards, he'll shake like the devil and spray water for ten feet around. Heck, I could rent him to a cleaning company to use as a high-pressure hose."

Socrates brayed, reminding her she had work to attend to. "I think that's dry enough. Brody, do you have—"

Before she could finish, he handed her a piece of clean plywood. "He can stand on this while you do the other front hoof. Let them both dry for a while, then do the back hooves."

"I'm assuming you forgot that I grew up with animals," she grumbled, trying not to pay any attention to the man who commanded it, even when giving a skunk a bath. She carefully polished the other hoof, then braided the mule's mane. That done, she stood back, studying her work with a critical eye. "Not much tail here, buddy. I'll just comb it out and fluff it up a bit."

Her mom, swinging competently on her crutches under Luke's watchful gaze, negotiated the grass between the Oinkari Basque Dancers Booth and Brody's rig. "I'm going to take a nap, so I'd appreciate it if you two would get whatever you need out of the camper."

"I have my stuff stowed in the trailer, so I'm good." Brody faced Rita. "You?"

"Just a few things. Be right back." Judy didn't look a bit tired to her.

Just as Rita closed the camper door, her mom smiled and pointed to a package beside the tire. "Wait a minute. There are a few more things you might need."

Rita raised her eyebrows. "I can't think of anything else. I have a change of clothes and my makeup."

"I had Luke bring your old rodeo clothes. Boots, hat, spurs. You can wear your jeans, but I brought along a new western shirt—you've filled out on top some—and a scarf."

"Mom, my days of dressing like a cowgirl are over. I'm Vice President of International Operations for Pettybottham Enterprises now."

Judy, with her slightly opened mouth and frown, looked so hurt that Rita took the clothes.

"Thanks, I'll think about it."

Chapter 9

I knew I was right. I could spend the rest of my life with Rita grooming me and die a happy mule. That girl has the magic touch, for sure. She didn't brush the hair on my ears the wrong way, which is a plus, and I've never had such shiny hooves. I look fabulous.

So now I'm even more committed to persuading Brody to propose. And convincing her to agree—which might be an even higher fence to jump. The only way to overcome the objections of two obstinate people is to be even more obstinate than they are. That's a tough project, but I'm unflinching in my dedication to the task.

Perseus is excited about the shows this weekend. What a vain dog, always wanting to be the center of attention. He has barked his displeasure over the acquisition of the baby porcupine, though, woofing about the future possibility of quills in his nose. I told him to keep his nose where it belongs and he won't have to worry.

Speaking of the shows, Beauty has her tail out of joint because she wants to perform, too. I tried to tell her that she hasn't rehearsed an act, but she's smugly insisting that with her half-bloodhound/half-collie good looks, she doesn't need an act. I, of course, think she's just jealous, but she might as well go with Perseus as long as she stays away from the livestock.

Guinevere has been uncharacteristically silent, although the silly skunk is prone to stage fright, so maybe that's her problem. I'm in the middle of the show here, so won't need reports from the others.

As for the progress of Rita and Brody's romance, I'll let you judge for yourself. While I'd like things to happen a little faster, you can only expect so much from humans, especially those who are as thickskulled as my two. Notice I'm claiming Rita now. Really, I don't think it's too soon. In fact, I plan to use my own charming good looks to lure her closer to Brody.

Many opportunities await, and Perseus, Guinevere, and Beauty are willing to go to any length to see their goals accomplished. And just maybe, with love in the air for Judy and Luke, Brody and Rita will see the light.

As Rita put the finishing touches on Socrates' tail, a teenaged girl shyly approached.

"Are you Rita Markum?"

"I am." She smiled, hoping to put the girl at ease. "Are you having fun at the rodeo?"

"You got that right. My name's Dani Baker. You might remember my mom, Karla Harris?"

"Oh, yes! She was rodeo queen when I was about your age and I wanted to be just like her. She gave me lots of tips and tricks, and helped me win, too. What a lovely woman, your mother is."

The tips of the girl's mouth turned down. "Was. Car wreck."

A pang pierced Rita's heart at the loss of her old friend. She should have known. But when Karla's family was in need, she'd been in Seattle pursuing her career. Rita realized that her priorities had changed considerably in the last ten years, and her idea of what was important needed some serious rethinking. "I'm so sorry."

Dani shrugged in that pubescent I-can-handle-anything way kids do when you've gotten too close to their feelings. "Me, too." She pointed to a sleek bay gelding that undoubtedly had thoroughbred blood in him. "That's my barrel horse, Zoomer."

"He's beautiful."

"I've been training him to run the barrels all summer and he's ready to go, except I had an appendectomy last week and

Dad won't let me ride yet. But Zoomer really, really needs to run in front of a loud audience to help him get ready for next year and this is his last chance."

"That's too bad." She meant it. He was built to run, and performing in front of an audience would be an important part of his training.

The girl trailed the toe of her boot in the dirt. "So I was wondering, uh, since my mom said you could ride like the wind and all, that, uh, if you'd take him out. I'm already entered and everything and the judge said you could take my place." Her words tumbled out faster. "I know you haven't been around for a while, but you could practice on him. It would be fun!"

Definitely not. Rita's rodeoing days were over, but she didn't want to hurt this girl's feelings, either. "I just can't, honey. I haven't been on a horse for a long time—so long ago, I bet you weren't even walking yet." A horse like that would probably dump her on her kiester at the first turn.

Tears welled in Dani's eyes but she blinked them away. "Okay, no problem."

Rita relaxed her throat, hoping the lump would go away. She didn't have any business at all getting on a barrel racing horse with no conditioning whatsoever. Still, Dani had been through enough hurt already. But no.

"Can you ask someone else?"

"I already have." Dani grinned bravely. "Be sure to get a chorizo at our 4-H booth."

"I sure will." Rita had eaten in fine restaurants all over the country, but not one thing was better than a genuine Basque chorizo on a hotdog bun. Supporting Dani's 4-H group wouldn't be a stretch.

After the girl left, Rita felt like a Class-A louse. She headed straight for the chorizos, bought four of them, and brought them back to the camper. Brody had already donned his greasepaint —a white face with an exaggerated, red smile, green nose to match his derby, and a black circle around his right eye.

Brody's camper was one of several lined up on the side of the pasture at the end of the arena. Most of the campers that pulled horse trailers were owned by ropers and bulldoggers, but some roughstock riders hauled horses around, too. Many had wives or daughters who barrel raced, and some trained roping horses.

Fifty feet opposite the campers, community groups had set up their vending booths. You could buy everything from the aforementioned chorizos, to saddles, to a palm reading.

"It's Brody Alexander!" a girl shrieked, a fresh cherry Sno Cone in her hand. She led the pack to him and asked him to sign their shirts. One wanted her bum signed, but he shook his head.

"I'll be at the dance tonight, Brody," Sno Cone girl said. "If you come, I'll have a special treat for you!"

Special treat, my patootie. Or hers, rather. Rita's blood boiled. They had no right!

Bum Girl piped up, "I'll be in the barrel racing, and if I win, I'll give you my buckle."

"You better keep your buckle." He tipped his hat. "When you're eighty, your seventy-five-year-old boyfriend will want to look at it."

"Eeeeew!" all three chorused.

Marching directly into the fray, Rita shoved a chorizo at him. "Mom's waiting for you in the camper." She grabbed his sleeve and pulled. Luckily, he followed. "Nice little fan club you have there."

Shrugging, he knocked on the camper. "It goes with the territory."

"Why are you knocking on your own door?"

He grinned. "That goes with the territory, too."

Luke swung the door open. "C'mon in."

Rita practically shoved Brody in, then, looking behind her to make sure those bucklebunnies noticed, followed him.

He handed the chorizo back to her. "Looks good, but I can't eat before a show. I'll take about a dozen of them afterwards, though." He winked at her. "Nice girls here."

"Hrmph. Easy girls here."

"I'll bet they look good in the saddle."

"Probably so, but they're jailbait."

"True. That's why I avoid them."

"You call that *avoiding*? I don't call that avoiding. I'm surprised you didn't sign that girl's hiney."

Judy hid her mouth with her hand, but Rita could see her eyes twinkling. Luke didn't bother hiding anything—he tipped his head back and laughed.

Furious, Rita grabbed her hat, boots, and spurs from the top of her cot. "See you later."

It had been so long since she'd ridden a horse that Rita nearly forgot how to buckle her spurs.

"Thanks, so much, Rita. I owe you one!" All smiles, Dani slipped the bit into Zoomer's mouth. "Even riding him for practice will be good because he'll get used to someone else. He's only been around me."

Great. The first time she'd been on a horse in over ten years, and it had to be a spirited racer who'd never been ridden by anyone other than his owner. "I'll take it easy with him, then let him go a little faster." She hoped she sounded confident. "Then I'll take him around the barrels full-tilt."

"Sounds good. You can still ride in the competition tonight, too, if you change your mind."

"I won't."

Dani smiled again. A knowing smile.

But the girl was wrong, Rita vowed. She wouldn't change her mind—she couldn't possibly ride in the actual race. She'd make a dang fool of herself, racing with no conditioning, and she already felt uncomfortable enough wearing her high school get-up. Probably get dumped on her pockets right in front of Brody.

After a final adjustment of her spurs and a tug of her scarf, she squirted half a can of hairspray on her hair, put on her old

Stetson, and pinned it tight to her hair. Just like the old days, except then, she'd have hairsprayed her eye makeup, too. Made it stay on longer.

"I'm ready if Zoomer is."

"Zoomer's always ready. He'll take me all the way to the national finals—you'll see."

Rita patted Zoomer on the neck. Her assessment of his conformation left her no doubt this horse had the capability. "I bet he will. You just keep working him." She took the reins in one hand, put the toe of her boot in the stirrup, and swung on. "Work him every day, without fail."

The gelding stood about sixteen hands, maybe a little more. Rita had forgotten how high you were, how far you could see, and how powerful you felt with twelve-hundred pounds of lean-muscled horse between your legs. "Let's go." She nudged Zoomer to walk to the barrels.

First she walked all the way around the practice pasture, then she trotted him.

"I'll take him for a spin, now. Is he right or left?"

Dani beamed with pride. "Left."

Rita trotted him around the barrels. It all seemed so natural, including the struggle to hold him back on the home stretch, that it seemed as if she hadn't missed a day of training. "Okay, he's warmed up. I'm going to run him."

"Just hang on, Rita. He'll hug those barrels so tight your leg will have to turn into an overcooked noodle to get by."

"That's what I like to hear." Zoomer tugged at the bit, anxious to run. She hunkered down and reined him back, then spurred him toward the first barrel. He took off like a shot. Her leg rammed the first barrel, knocking it down. On to the second. Made that one. Third barrel, she'd figured out Zoomer's rhythm and they skimmed it perfectly. Home stretch, she gave him his head and leaned over to enjoy the ride.

She pulled over to the grinning owner of a very fine horse, and smiled down at the girl. "You're right, you've got a winner, Dani, and you've done a heckuva job training him. I'm really proud of you. Your appendix sure picked a bad time to need removing."

"No kidding, and thanks. I work him a couple of hours every day. He shied at the barrels at first, but he's fine now. Don't know what he'll do on the barrels they have in the arena, though. He's always run these orange ones, and those are Coors cans."

"He might surprise you." Zoomer side-stepped back toward the barrels, wanting to run again.

"Would you run him for me? Please? And the Grand Entry, too. There'll be a lot of noise then and it'll be good for him."

"I don't suppose it would hurt if I rode him then, but I still don't want to ride in competition." At the girl's fallen expression, Rita reiterated, "I haven't ridden for a long, long time, Dani. Competition is no place to start. I probably won't even be able to walk tomorrow."

"Why don't you take him around again before he cools off?"

Rita knew she should dismount right then and let it go, but she didn't want to leave the saddle just yet.

"As smooth as this horse runs, it'd be my pleasure." She rode back to the starting position and Dani waved the flag to start, this time running the stop watch. Zoomer made the run in less than twenty seconds, about two seconds over the runs in competition. He'd never win unless he cut a couple of seconds off that time. "Let's try it again."

She made a few adjustments during the next three runs until Zoomer finished in under nineteen seconds. She swung out of the saddle and handed the reins to Dani. "He's an athlete, he's got try, and you've trained him well—just pull him up a bit at the second barrel because he's anticipating." Rita patted the horse on the neck. "You definitely have a winner here. I'll be back fifteen minutes before Grand Entry."

After making her escape, Rita had to dodge a couple of horses that nearly ran her over. "Watch where you're going!"

She turned her gaze in the direction of the riders—the same girls who'd been flirting with Brody—to see the object of their affections doing his stretches. "Good grief."

"Sorry, ma'am," one girl said.

The *ma'am* got to Rita. Twenty-eight wasn't *that* old. "You're excused. But try to use a little caution on the rodeo grounds, even when you're ogling the bullfighter."

The girls giggled. The one who'd asked him to sign her derriere said, "Brody told us he'd dance three times with the winning barrel racer tonight—that's going to be *me*."

Rita ground her teeth, not believing that he'd actually dance with jailbait. What was he thinking? And anyway, he'd already asked her, not that she'd given him a definite answer . . .

At that moment, her skin chilled. She knew. She understood the pressure Brody had borne all along, and how uncomfortable he'd been with the attentions of young girls. She'd been one of them, and she was sorry not only for adding to his difficulties, but for being so selfish that she'd completely misjudged him. He was an honorable man.

A quick one-eighty and she found Dani and Zoomer in no time. "I'll run him. But be there when I fall on my ass."

Dani giggled. "You won't fall. You have a good, solid seat. I could learn a few things from you."

"And a few things not to do, too," Rita muttered.

Brody admired Rita's tight Levi's and what they held as she dodged some horses, had a few words with the girls who'd been bothering him, then hurried back to the horse she'd run the barrels on. He'd watched her runs, and my-oh-my, what a seat. The rest of her wasn't too shabby, either.

What had her in such a snit, he couldn't guess. The glare she shot him and the way she swung her arms as she took long strides back to the practice course left no doubt but what he was in deep doo-doo for something. But he had no time for distractions. He continued his stretches, checked his animals, and put on his game face.

The stock contractor, Jim Jensen, came over and handed him the list of bulls. "Rascal's here."

"No problem."

"I seem to recall you had a problem with him in Winnemucca."

"Taught me to pay attention, is all." By poking a horn through his ribs. He'd ended up in the hospital for a week with a lacerated liver for that little episode. He tucked the list in his shirt pocket. "Good stock. Oughta be some decent scores."

"Just keep 'em spinning." Jim slapped him on the shoulder. "Have a good show."

The girls rode by on their way to the Grand Entry. "Put on your dancin' shoes—I'll be ready for you, Brody!" the pushy one said, sending him what she probably thought was a seductive smile. Heck, in ten years she'd be quite a looker.

Never knowing what to do with these girls, he smiled halfheartedly, sending them into a fit of giggles. While his ego didn't mind the flattery, teenagers couldn't hold a candle to a woman who knew the score. Like Rita.

But he didn't want to hurt the girls' tender feelings, either. He had to deal with the problem as best he could every single show, while trying not to let it interfere with his concentration. It was one part of the job he could do without. Now, the twenty-something bucklebunnies were a different story.

Another barrel racer trotted by. He caught a glance of her tush and his interest heightened. Rita? He shook his head. That woman held more surprises than a case of Cracker Jacks. As he stretched his back and shoulder muscles, he enjoyed the nice fit of her rear in the saddle until she rode out of sight.

The announcer began the proceedings, so Brody gathered his animals and headed for the arena. He was always the last one announced, and he liked to make an entertaining entrance. As he heard his name called, he sprinted into the arena, Perseus doing flips, Guinevere flitting her tail and drawing titters, and Socrates trailing, stealing the handkerchiefs from his back pocket. It was a crowd pleaser.

Then came more laughter. He turned to see Beauty trotting behind Socrates, holding his scrawny tail in her mouth like elephants do. Brody patted the ugly-but-cute dog on the head. What the heck, she deserved her fifteen minutes of fame.

The audience stood for a scratchy recording of *The Star-Spangled Banner* while the flag bearers raced around the arena in opposite directions, the same way he'd seen a thousand times. The announcer thanked the contestants and they formed a single line, waving to the crowd while they raced around the arena once before exiting.

The one contestant who drew the most applause was Rita Markum. He put his hat over his heart and donned his most lovesick expression as she galloped by, eliciting laughter from the kids and cheers from the adults.

What wasn't there to love about rodeo?

He helped with the kids' steer riding, then, between the saddlebronc and barrel racing, did his animal act. For the jillionth time, he told the joke, "My mama won't let me go to California."

"Why's that?" the announcer asked.

"She's worried I might fall into bad company."

"Bad company, huh?"

"Yeah, she overheard some people talkin' about all them sunny-beaches they had down there."

The kids howled and the parents chuckled at their kids' laughter. As far as Brody was concerned, rodeo was all about kids—giving them some good, wholesome fun.

Then Socrates dropped a fake firecracker down his baggies, which blew them off, and Brody ran out of the arena rubbing his butt. The kids howled with laughter as the animals trailed him, but now he was in his bullfighting get-up.

While the barrel racing took place, Luke and Judy met him and took the animals. Brody stayed by the chutes and joked with the nervous bullriders while stretching his legs and pumping himself up for cowboy protection. He'd be the only bullfighter there, so a hung-up cowboy could get dicey. But what a rush.

He heard the announcer praise the time of the one girl he'd hoped would tip over a barrel.

"And that little lady has the lead with eighteen-point-nine seconds. Man, was she ever flyin'!" the announcer called.

Dang, she had the fastest time. Two riders left to go. He wondered if he could get the stomach flu or something so he didn't have to make an appearance at the dance. The next racer knocked over a barrel for a five-second penalty.

Then the announcer said, "Well, lookee here. For the first time in ten years we have a Markum. You might recall her daddy—one of our top roughstock riders for years and the circuit bullriding champion for three years running. Last time we saw this lady, she was Owyhee County Rodeo Queen and had won every barrel racing competition around, so you folks are in for quite a treat. She's riding a horse owned and trained by Dani Baker. Here she is, Miss Rita Markum!"

Fool that she was, she'd agreed to Dani's pleas to race Zoomer. But only because she finally realized Brody didn't welcome the attentions of his groupies, and that ten years ago, she'd put him in the very same, uncomfortable position.

And, okay, she loved to race.

Hearing her name boom out of the ancient speakers made her heart thump, her muscles tense, and her vision sharpen. She hadn't felt this alive in years. Zoomer, alarmed at all the noise, reared, then pranced sideways. She reined the excited gelding in, backed him up, then nodded when she had him in position. Zoomer trembled, born to race, ready to go.

The judge flagged her to start. She nudged her spurs into his side and pulled leather, praying he'd take the first barrel tight, but not too close. She reined him in a few feet in the approach, then let him make his turn. The barrel banged into her shin and wobbled. She didn't look back. If it fell over, the crowd would tell her soon enough.

He took the second barrel like a champ, sprinted for the third barrel. Again, she banged her shin—in the same place. She ignored the pain. The crowd roared as she leaned forward and spurred Zoomer down the home stretch. The judge flagged her finish with a flourish. Pulling up, she couldn't help grinning like an idiot. Her heart swelled with pride and she fought back tears. Columns of numbers could never compete with running the barrels.

They paid a whole lot better, though.

"Eeeighteeeen and threeeee!" the announcer called over the cheers and applause. "Folks, give your winner a big hand. Rita Markum, our homegrown, champion cowgirl!"

Rita took her victory lap around the arena, waving to the audience, fighting back the tears. Too many memories, too much fun. Maybe she should have taken a page from her father's book instead of opting for the corporate mold.

She galloped Zoomer out of the arena, past the chutes.

"Nice seat, pretty lady," Brody called.

Reining the gelding to a sliding stop, she grinned down at him. "Does this mean I get to dance with you, cowboy?"

The bullriders hooted and whistled.

"Anywhere, anytime, sweetheart." He winked and lowered his voice. "And thanks. I was dreading the danged dance a lot more than old Rascal."

"I finally figured that out."

A bull reared in the shoot, commanding everyone's attention for a moment. In a louder voice he said, "Gotta go." He cocked his head toward the bullpen and grinned. "My fan club's waiting."

Rita thoroughly enjoyed the bullriding event and Brody's handling of the big animals. The next rider bucked off, but his hand was trapped in the bullrope. The bull flung the man around like a rag doll. Her heart nearly stopped, fearing for both the bullrider's safety and knowing what Brody would do next.

He thrived on danger, just like all the other men she'd known until she moved to the city.

Fearless, daring, and downright foolhardy, Brody rushed to the side of the bull, jumped up, and jerked the bullrope's tail, releasing the hung cowboy's hand from the bull. The cowboy flew several feet in the air and landed off to the side like a sack of potatoes.

The bull whipped around and bashed Brody in the ribs with one huge horn. Even though Brody's ribs were probably broken, he kept the animal away from the downed cowboy until the chute crew could drag the unconscious man off to the ambulance. Finally, the pick-up men herded the snorting bull back into the corral.

Rita had seen this same scenario, and worse, time and time again. It's what bullfighters did. She wanted him to leave the arena and get medical attention, only imagining what her friends at Pettybottham would think. They'd think he was deranged or had a death wish. Parachuting off the Space Needle was safer, and those who pulled that stunt were arrested.

Brody bent slightly and pressed his cast into his side, then got into position for the next bull. Rita knew he was in pain, but she also knew he wouldn't quit. A man like him didn't quit unless he had a bone sticking out of his leg or was unconscious, simple as that.

In a way, she admitted her admiration for these men, but in practical terms, she couldn't abide it.

Ten rides, ten lucky cowboys—even the one who was hurt would have been in a lot worse shape if it hadn't been for Brody's willingness to take a painful hit to protect the rider.

Rita was relieved when the last and meanest bull, Rascal, didn't cause any problems. The kids laughed hysterically when Brody called, "Here kitty, kitty!" and pawed the dirt, imitating the bull. Rascal finally decided he wanted to eat more than he wanted to trample and gore the bullfighter, so ambled lazily out of the arena.

Overall, it had been a heckuva show, and Rita couldn't have been more proud of Brody. Still she hurried to the chutes to see if he'd broken his ribs.

As she got there, a paramedic ran his hand along Brody's side, poking and prodding. "One, maybe two cracked ribs. You should get an x-ray to be sure. A couple more bruised pretty bad. I'll tape you up."

"Naw, I'll do it. Thanks. See you tomorrow night." He shook the man's hand.

Brushing the back of Rita's waist, he nudged her toward the camper. "How about you and me dance under the stars tonight?"

She leaned into his good side as they walked. With his sore ribs, she didn't think he'd be doing much dancing. "Mmmm, sounds like a plan. Are you on jailbait alert?"

"That I am. But you saved me."

"Looked like you needed a little saving."

"Every show." He sighed. "It's hard, because I don't want to hurt their feelings, but. . ."

"But they won't stop."

He nodded, then grinned. "I don't want to stop one of those bucklebunnies."

Rita was a bit taken back. Didn't he just say he needed rescuing? "The one who wanted you to sign her rear end?"

"No, the one in tight Levi's who showed those baby girls how to run the barrels."

She pretended to sock him in the shoulder. "You can't have my buckle, though."

"Huh?"

"Does this make you a buckle-buck? You know, the male equivalent?"

"Darlin', you can keep your buckle. I just want to undo it."

Oh, and she wanted him to unbuckle it, too. It was very unwise, of course, and odds were high she'd regret it, but odds were higher she'd regret never being with him.

"How're the ribs?"

146

"Let's just say you should probably be on top."

"Oh." Translation: they hurt like hell.

Brody groaned when he climbed the steep steps of the camper and there was nothing she could do to help him. He sat at the kitchen table and she sat opposite him. In the middle of the table lay a note with 'Rita' written on it in her mother's handwriting. She opened the note and read it, then when she managed to catch a short breath, glanced up at Brody. "Mom and Luke caught a ride home with a friend—says she was tired. Told me not to worry because she took Mrs. Pretty Bottom."

Brody stood and squeezed by her and the miniature kitchen sink, his grunt barely audible. Still she knew he was in pain.

"I need my ribs wrapped before another minute goes by." He fished around in the dinky bathroom cabinet and found some vet tape. "I hope Judy didn't overdo."

As if fighting bulls after he cracked his ribs wasn't overdoing.

"I think she did," Rita said, trying to sound nonchalant, both about her mom's full-blossom romance, and the thought of touching Brody's bare skin. "She also says Luke proposed and she agreed."

"Good. They've been flirting with each other for years."

"More than you know. The other day she told me they dated before she married my dad."

He brushed a stray lock from Rita's forehead. "So are you hot and bothered she's marrying an old, busted-up bullrider?"

"Just hot and bothered." Rita unsnapped his shirt, pulled out the shirttails, and ran her hands over the scars on his washboard abs. "I'll wrap those ribs for you, cowboy."

"I'd like you to wrap those legs of yours around me." He caught her chin with the tip of his finger, and slowly lowered his lips to hers. His kiss sizzled, her lips welcomed his as he touched her with his tongue. Her breasts became oversensitive, aching for his touch, but still he kissed her, so powerful he was a little scary, yet so magnetic she couldn't draw away if she wanted to.

She ran her fingers through his hair, still sweaty from his performance. He was hot, tired, and hurting—not necessarily in that order. The problem was, she was hot, too. For him. Right now. But first things first.

With a step back, she held out her hand. "Hand me the vet tape."

He did, then winced as he shrugged off his shirt.

Rita hadn't taped anyone up since her dad had died, but she still remembered how. She used the moment to get a grip on her emotions and to tell her body to calm down, although she doubted her body would ever be calm around Brody Alexander.

After she found the end of the tape and peeled off a little, she said, "Suck in your breath halfway and hold it."

"I can't hold my breath—you take it away."

She knew the feeling, and worse. Her teenage heart had ached with love for him, even while thinking he didn't love her back. A man who didn't flinch when a bull bashes into his ribs, who was still recovering from a broken arm and a bum leg, and who would soon have other injuries, maybe slight, maybe life-threatening. A mere woman could never, ever top the endorphin rush of man against beast.

Still, she couldn't help but try. The thrill of conquering a man who'd yet to be bested was alluring, but when that man was Brody Alexander, it was irresistible.

"Lift your arms."

When he did, she made quick work of taping him, thoroughly but not too tightly. When she finished, she leaned forward and kissed his chest.

"Now, where were we, mighty bullfighter man who knows no pain?"

"Oh, I know pain. Every time you leave me I know pain."

He hadn't given her a second thought all these years and she knew it. For now, she had business to tend to. "Odds are . . ."

"Odds are high that I'm going to kiss you, Rita. Look into my eyes, be with me."

She tipped her face toward him. "I'd say the chances are pretty close to a hundred percent."

"I'm going to make love to you, Rita. I've wanted you for years, but never like I want you this moment."

Oh, how she loved hearing those words and the sexy growl of his voice.

He drew her into his arms, not hard, just enough to share his courage and strength—enough to make her body mold to his, seeking his heat, her own need soaring beyond numbers and odds. Her heart beat faster and she wondered why she so desperately wanted him, why her heart wouldn't listen to her head.

Neither did her body, for when he took off her shirt and unclasped her bra, the appreciative glint in his eye made her lose all reason.

"You're so much more than I dreamed." He bent down and drew his lips around her nipple. Rita drew in a sharp breath as he made electricity charge from her breasts to between her legs. He flicked the other nipple with his fingers, intensifying her pleasure to nearly the point of unbearable sensations. But she needed more.

He stopped, then held her face in both of his hands. "Rita, I'm going to back you up to my cot, but I wasn't joking when I said you'd need to be on top. I know it sounds coarse and very unromantic, but . . ."

"Hush." She put her forefinger to his lips. "Let's get some of those clothes off you, starting with your cleats."

"There's scissors in the silverware drawer. I have to knot my shoestrings so they don't come untied in the arena."

Rita made quick work of cutting his laces. He toed off his shoes and kicked them under the bed. Then he reached for her waist and unbuckled her belt.

"Ah, here's the real prize, *under* the buckle."

"Took you long enough to figure that out."

"I'm a slow learner."

She shoved his clown shorts down. "I'm not."

Brody stepped out of his shorts and took off his athletic cup. His shaft was as magnificent as the rest of him. She reached to take him in her hand, wanting to feel his hardness, but he stopped her. "In time, darlin'. Be patient."

He sat on the bed pulling her with him, slid his hands up her thighs to her waist, and kissed her belly. And kissed lower, kissing and licking, great pleasure to come. The anticipation was killing her. She could barely breathe or move, lest she spoil the moment. He slid her Wranglers over her hips, and she savored the sensation of his rough palms on her smooth flesh.

She couldn't resist brushing her hands along his shoulders and down his chest to his six-pack abs. His sharp intake of breath showed he was as hot for her as she was for him. Then again, his arousal was obvious. Rita wanted to give him a ride he wouldn't forget anytime soon.

Five second's worth of sanity crept in, and she realized if she made love to him, it really would be love. That she'd give her whole heart to him, and she'd never get it back. But then she'd given her heart to him years ago. That's why she could never love David the way she loved Brody. Love couldn't be quantified, qualified, or trapped in a barrel. Love did what it did, and she loved Brody.

Rita crawled on the bed and pushed him back. He oomphed at the impact.

"Sorry about those ribs, but you'll just have to forget about them for a few minutes."

She felt like a wanton woman, hovering over him. The aggressor. He reached up and caressed her breasts, then tugged gently on her nipples. She was under his spell, ready to give him everything he wanted, and more.

"You make me crazy, woman." He cocked his head toward a drawer beside the bed. "Protection's in there."

While she took care of the deed, he drove her crazy by running his fingers through her womanly folds and when he teased her sensitive clitoris, she nearly came undone.

"So hot you are, Rita. Open up for me—let me in."

"Don't buck me off, cowboy."

"Odds are pretty low. Now please, I'm begging."

The set of his jaw didn't look much like begging, more like demanding. She couldn't ever imagine this man begging. It might be fun to see if she could make that happen sometime, though. Or better yet, make him lose his heart to her the way she had lost hers to him.

"The chute's opening, cowboy. Let out the bull." With a throaty laugh, she slid up on him, then down, taking him in part way. She closed her eyes and waited until she could comfortably accommodate him, even as wet as she was, then took a little more of him.

Brody groaned, his body twitching in anticipation.

"Hold on. It's your turn to be patient."

Finally, she started moving, first only slightly, then more, then she was able to feel the fullness of his erection all the way inside. She thought she'd lose it right there, but wanted to delay her climax for him.

When he massaged her breasts and tweaked her nipples, she nearly came unglued. The primal force urged her to move faster, to take all of him she could. He was moving, too, even with his cracked ribs. The pressure built, she could think of nothing, see nothing, only taste him, and feel him.

The fireworks started and she wanted it to last forever, wanted to stay with him forever. Wanted him and only him forever.

He roared his own release, his eyes dark with passion, sweat beading on his brow.

"Rita, you are a wonder."

She leaned over and kissed him tenderly on the lips. His hands rested on her derriere. She'd been right. This was wrong. Now, she'd never get her heart back. And Brody would still be Brody, traveling down the road year in and year out, teasing bulls, getting injured, and partying on Saturday night.

Did he even know he owned her heart? A tear welled in her eye, but she refused to let it come to the surface.

He kissed her back. "That was a heck of an hors d'oeuvres. I'll never be able get enough of you."

"We are good together, aren't we?"

"Looks promising. I think we need more research." He kissed her again, only this one was a starting kiss, not a goodbye kiss.

They left for home directly after the second show at Rita's insistence. Brody would have preferred to spend the night— with her. The previous night had been one he'd only dreamed of before. He could easily spend his life with this woman.

"You awake?"

She straightened and fussed with her seatbelt. "Yes, just thinking."

"Me, too." He shot another glance at her then back to the road. "We make a good team, Rita."

"Don't go there."

"Why not?" he asked, against his better judgment.

"Because you're you and I'm me. I have a job waiting for me in Houston and I'll be there, in my office, in November. You're you, and you love your ranch almost as much as you love rodeoing. End of story."

He wondered what she'd think when he showed up for the annual board meeting in December. For her, it would almost be worth it to give up the life he'd built, go the easy route, get his girl and please his mother all in one shot. He pictured himself chained to his desk and his stomach lurched.

Bullfighting was his life. A man like him could never be happy for long stuck in an air-conditioned office in a plastic building for long. She knew it, and he knew it.

"Just a thought, was all."

She reached over and massaged his arm. "For the record, I love you. I've loved you since I was jailbait."

His heart thumped and he couldn't help grinning. "For the

record, I would have walked on hot coals to be with you that night, but sixteen is too young for a girl to get involved in hanky-panky." He knew she remembered the night he referred to by the guilty half-smile on her face.

"I know that now."

"So if you love me, why did you take up with David?"

She shrugged. "Because he was safe. The most dangerous thing he does is dodge in-line skaters at Greenlake."

Brody stared at the passing stripes on the road. "For the record, I've loved you since you were jail bait."

Leaning her head back, she closed her eyes. "But it was never meant to be."

He saw one tear pool in her eye.

Chapter 10

Ha! I knew it all along. Rita and Brody are in love.

Were it dignified for a mule to do a happy dance, I'd be doing one. Surely that wedding ring will find its way onto the fourth finger of Rita's left hand soon.

Yes, they think they have insurmountable problems. Humans, shortsighted as they are, can rarely work their way through a dilemma without first digging themselves into some sort of a trauma. It's one of those puzzling things I've observed that only humans would do. Not even porcupines are that boneheaded.

Oh, and didn't you think Beauty did a great job with the Grand Entry? After I get the humans situated, I'll start lobbying for her to join our show. She's a natural. I'd compare her to Kathy Griffin with slobbers.

But back to the primary objective. I heard Judy tell Luke that she's going to organize a house-raising party next weekend. Everyone will be there, and I think it would be great opportunity for Brody and Rita to announce their engagement. They're not engaged, you say? We have six days to work on that little tripping point.

Speaking of porcupines, Mrs. Pretty Bottom seems to be here to stay whether we like it or not. I told the others that they might as well get used to the idea because I saw Rita trying to teach it tricks. I'm here to tell you that if a porcupine had brains, it wouldn't need quills. Rita has her work cut out for her.

A dozen families, some living as far as thirty miles away, had gathered, bringing hammers, saws, tape measures, and lots of food. Besides the men, the younger women had their own tool belts and would work on the house, too. The older ladies and children would serve the food.

Rita handed her mom a large glass of ice tea while Judy and Luke accepted the congratulations of their friends.

"We drove to Murphy and bought our wedding license this morning," Judy told them.

"I thought we better get it before she changed her mind." They laughed at Luke's comment, but Rita didn't think he was joking.

Brody walked toward her. "You plan to eat all this?"

Rita smiled, taking a look at the three tables full of roast beef, homemade bread, and pies. Jell-O salads of every imaginable color lined one side of the foundation they'd poured next to the Pie Palace a couple years earlier. "I might need a little help. When's the truck due?"

"In a few minutes. The driver just called on the cell phone."

"Maybe he'll be hungry." She'd never been good at small talk, and awkward silence hovered between them after the intimate conversation a few days earlier. She wished things could be different. She wished she could stay.

"You fit in here. You ought to stay." Apparently, Brody's thoughts had taken the same turn.

She shook her head and fussed with the napkin arrangement. "Mom will need all the financial assistance I can give her if Luke's old injuries flare up. I don't dare even consider turning down the job at Pettybottham Enterprises." She gazed up at him. "Besides, I've worked hard for that company. I enjoy it."

"And you're good at it."

She nodded. "*Very* good at it."

Luckily, two trucks loaded with building supplies pulled up at that moment, sending dust swirling over the food, all fortunately still covered with plastic wrap. Just when the dust settled, another truck arrived with the trusses.

Turning to her, Brody outlined her jaw with his finger. "Time to get to it." He picked up the architectural drawings propped up beside the table and tucked them under his arm, then called to the other men, "Let's get this thing unloaded. With luck, we'll have the whole house framed and roofed by the end of the day." He fired up the air compressor. "Would you get the nail guns out of the shed?"

"Thanks for renting them," she said, heading toward Phyllis' tool shed. "They'll speed things up quite a bit." But even with nail guns and fifteen workers, framing and roofing a five-bedroom house in a single day seemed pretty ambitious.

As she brought the first armload of nail guns out of the shed, Brody sent her a heart-melting smile. But then, her heart always melted at the very sight of him. She yearned for the life that could have been.

By mid-afternoon, she had to admit that his leadership skills and the hardworking enthusiasm of the men had shown her wrong. While the hot sun beat down, shirts came off, but the nail guns Brody had rented never stopped banging. Rita worried about Brody's fractured arm and ribs, but he worked as hard and long as anyone, even though they often urged him to take five.

Wives and children made sure their men had water every half-hour, and they'd all taken a twenty-minute break at noon. Meantime, a truck had delivered the roofing materials, and another delivered windows and doors.

By now, they'd finished the framing. Most of the men worked on the roofing, the rest installing foam board.

"Not bad for a bunch of local ranchers."

Startled at Brody's voice, she would have been able to control the flush creeping up her cheeks had he not handed her a little bouquet of dandelions.

"Uh, thank you." She buried her nose in the fragrant flowers, breathing deeply. "The ladies have planned a celebration for the opening of the children's home. I heard someone say it'll double as a wedding reception for Mom and Luke."

"Sounds like a happy way for the home to begin." He wiped the sweat from his forehead with his sleeve.

"Yes, but I won't be here then."

He slid his arm around her waist and pulled her to the tool shed, out of eyesight of most of the crew. "What could convince you to stay?"

"Pettybottham Enterprises moving their headquarters here."

Smirking, he said offhandedly, "I'll speak with the owners about that."

Rita laughed at his audacity. "I'm sure they'll be impressed."

"Aw, heck. Here comes Socrates."

She looked in the direction of Brody's gaze. The little mule trotted toward them as if on a mission. "Doesn't he ever stay home?"

Sighing, Brody shook his head. "Not if he doesn't want to."

"You rotten mule!" Rita pounded on the shed door. "Someone let us out!"

In the darkness behind her, Brody said, "I don't think they'll hear you with all those nail guns chattering like an orchestra of jack hammers."

Turning around, she sagged against the door. The shed had no windows, the only light coming from a small crack under the door. "Suggestions?"

"I'd try to break the door down, but my ribs don't like the idea."

"Neither would Phyllis."

"That, too." She heard him take a few steps and knock something over. "So far, I've identified a bucket, a shovel, and a lawnmower." After another clatter, he muttered, "Damn, and a garden rake. I'm gonna strangle that four-legged monster when I get out of here."

"We. When *we* get out of here."

She felt his nearness even before his arms slipped around her. "For now, we're stuck in a shed. Together." He kissed her forehead. "I suggest we make the most of it."

Her insides tightened with anticipation at the very thought. "Ah, but we can't. They could open the door at any time."

"And?" His breath on her neck made her toes tingle.

"And, uh, there are children out there."

Clearing his throat, he backed away a bit. "Right. Children." Then his arms enveloped her again. "We could give them kissing lessons."

"Lessons?" She wrapped her arms around him, taking care not to squeeze his ribs, and let him have his way with her mouth.

Several minutes and bone-melting kisses later, they sprang apart at the sound of the jiggling latch, but then the sound stopped. "Let us out," Rita yelled.

With a *clunk*, the door sprang open, flooding the shed with light, and Tommy peered in. "Ain't you a'skeered of the dark?"

She rushed outside and scooped the boy up in a big hug. "You're my hero! Brody and I were stuck in there and you saved us."

The boy's chest puffed out. "I'm gonna be a bullfighter when I grow up."

"Where's that danged mule," Brody muttered, blinking his eyes in the bright sunlight.

"Oh, he went home," Tommy said. Then, handing Brody the wedding ring set, he said, "But Socrates gave me this. I think I'm supposed to give it to you."

Brody took the ring and Rita was glad he refrained from saying the words she thought he was about to say. "If Socrates opened the door to the house, who knows where Perseus and Guinevere are by now." He stuck the ring in his pocket. "I better check to see if I have a ranch left."

He gave a five-dollar bill to Tommy. "Thanks for lending a helping hand, buddy."

Rita watched him stride all the way to his pickup—no one had a jaunty, self-confident stride like his. Each pace took him farther away from her, and her heart ached for him to be near her. Oh, how she wished things could be different.

"Mom, you're getting married," Rita reiterated, once again trying to convince Judy to be reasonable after driving nearly three hours to the Macy's in Karcher Mall. "A wedding dress is perfectly appropriate."

"I'm not an eighteen-year-old blushing bride. This dress looks too, well…virginal."

"Purity isn't measured in terms of sexual intercourse anymore. You're more pure at heart than anyone I know." Rita stood back and studied the lines of the gown. While not a perfect fit, the style flattered her mother's figure. "We'll put flowers in your hair instead of the veil."

Judy ran her hands over her silky hips. "Too tight here."

"We'll alter it."

"Too expensive."

"I have my credit card."

"Too pretentious."

"It's a very simple pattern."

"Too formal."

"Luke's eyeballs will pop out when he sees you."

"I'll take it." She turned to Rita. "I love it—it's just that I feel strange wearing it. I don't believe I've worn anything but jeans since the day you graduated from college—and that's the first dress I'd worn since your high school graduation. The same dress, actually."

"I know, but trust me on this one; you're beautiful in this gown."

Her mom smiled broadly, eyes shining, looking just like an eighteen-year-old blushing bride. "You'll need to get a fancy maid-of-honor gown so I won't show you up."

Laughing, Rita hugged her mother. "You'll show me up no

matter what I have on. You're the bride—you're supposed to."

Judy hugged her daughter back. "Let's go find some dresses for you to try on."

The week flew by. Rita pulled her Volvo in front of the Bruneau Community Church and turned to her mom. "We're here."

Fidgeting with her thumbnails, Judy nodded. "We were lucky the pastor had the afternoon available on such short notice."

"No time for small talk, Mom," Rita said as she cut the engine. "We have to start working on your clothes and war paint." She opened the door for Judy. After she'd helped her mom out, Rita got the dress bags and makeup case from the backseat.

"Whew!" Rita blew the bangs off her forehead. "Planning a wedding in six days has been a bit of a push. I just hope we've covered all of the bases."

"I called everyone I can think of."

"I hope you're set for clothing."

Judy nodded. "More clothes than I've ever had." They walked up the church steps. "Bless Phyllis' heart for insisting on taking charge of the cake and food. I think she helped poor Luke order the flowers, too."

The pastor welcomed them at the door and pointed them toward the ladies' dressing room.

"What'll we do for an entire hour?" Judy muttered. "I told you that was too much time—I'll just sit around and get nervous."

"You don't have to go through with this if you're having second thoughts."

"No, not second thoughts. I just get the willies when I have to stand up in front of a bunch of people, friends or not, and I'm afraid my voice won't work when I have to speak. Then Luke will think I don't want to get married, stomp out of the church, and leave me at the altar. Then when we get to the children's home, everyone will feel sorry for me and leave. A sorry sight—the food uneaten, the flowers wilted, a band with no one to play to, and an expensive honeymoon not used." She breathed in a deep sigh. "But that's silly."

"Yes, it is." Rita hugged her mom, who'd ditched her crutches a few days earlier in favor of a knee brace. "If Luke loves you as much as I think he does, a momentary stutter on your part won't make a bit of difference. In fact, he's probably worried about exactly the same thing."

"We should've gone to Reno and gotten married by an Elvis impersonator."

"Too late for that now. Besides, your wedding will be lovely, and you're beautiful. Can't you just wait to see Luke standing there, all gussied up, waiting for you?" But Rita envisioned Brody, not Luke, standing tall, his feet spread slightly, his broad shoulders drawn back. She licked her lips.

By then, she'd managed to maneuver Judy and all the paraphernalia into the dressing room. "Sit down, Mom," she said as she put the makeup case on the dressing table and hung their dresses on a hook high on the wall. "I'll do your makeup first, then mine. Then I'll do our hair. We won't put on our dresses until the last moment."

Phyllis joined them, breaking the tension with her lighthearted chatter.

An hour later, the first chords of the wedding march sounded. Rita, choked up and teary-eyed, had never seen her mother so brilliantly beautiful—or happy. She felt like a toad for ever opposing the match with Luke.

Phyllis slipped out quietly and sat with Tommy in the front pew. Rita grabbed her little bouquet, smoothed her blue A-line gown, and slowly walked down the aisle, hoping her mom would do okay unescorted, especially with her sore knee. But she had insisted.

At the sight of Brody, Rita's breath caught and her legs trembled just a bit. He gazed into her eyes, directly into her soul. She felt completely exposed to him, but not uncomfortably so. She only hoped she made it to the altar without making a fool of herself. He made a heartstoppingly dashing figure in a tux—sort of like a caged wild man who might escape and cause havoc at any moment.

She took her place opposite him and did her best to concentrate on her mother. Luke helped Judy up the two steps and never let go of her through the rest of the ceremony. Rita did her best to avoid eye contact with Brody, but couldn't resist sneaking glances at him every now and then, only to find him gazing right back at her.

"I pronounce you husband and wife," the pastor said. "Luke, you may now kiss your bride." Amidst loud cheers and applause, the couple kissed chastely. Rita knew her mom wouldn't be up to an intimate show, but that didn't mean they didn't love each other just as much.

Instructing them to turn toward the sanctuary, the pastor announced, "Folks, let me introduce Mr. and Mrs. Luke Bonner."

The organist struck up the music and Luke led Judy down the aisle. Brody offered Rita his arm and when she touched it, an electric current went straight to her heart.

Beauty nuzzled Brody's palm as he stood in front of the children's home. He was proud of the ranchers who'd worked so hard on it. Phyllis had decorated the unfinished building with flowers and silver bells. The overall effect was a bit garish—typically Phyllis. The guests loved it.

But now he had other worries—love was in the air at Grasmere, Idaho. Somehow, he had to get through the reception without making a fool of himself over the smartest, most beautiful woman he'd ever meet. And could never have.

His cell phone rang, and he groaned when he saw the number on Caller ID. He punched the *Talk* button with his thumb. "Hello, Mother."

"Good evening, Broderick. Were I to plan a little trip to Idaho, where might you recommend I go?"

His mother? In Idaho? "Sun Valley. Bring your skis. And wait until January."

"Been there years ago with your father. Lovely place. No, I was thinking more along the lines of something quaint, like Grasmere."

"Quit thinking about it, then. There are no beauty shops here, not a single art gallery, and the nearest Nordstrom is seven hours away. The nearest sidewalk is forty miles north and we have no electricity."

"What on earth do you do?"

"Hang out with nature. We have alkali dirt, sagebrush, and an infestation of Mormon crickets." He smiled when he imagined her shudder.

After a long silence, she said, "I'll bring bug spray."

She hung up, leaving him to wonder what scheme she had up her sleeve. He hoped she stayed in Houston where she belonged. But one thing he knew about his mother—she never, ever did what he wanted her to do.

Luke carried Judy toward the house, saying, "Ready to party?"

Judy giggled and beamed at her new husband. "I've got my dancin' shoes on."

Luke gave her a peck on the cheek. "I'm afraid you won't be dancing much tonight, Sugar. Not with that bum knee of yours."

Beauty sniffed Brody's camper. "Okay, I'll let your buddies out." He opened the door for the happy reunion. To Luke and Judy, he asked, "Where's Rita?"

"Home, pounding on her laptop. Mrs. Pettybottham called her on the cell phone asked for some information."

"Dang it all, Pettybottham Enterprises can wait until after the wedding reception."

"Exactly." She nodded toward the road. "Outta here. There's a damsel in distress twelve miles down the road."

"I'll take my trusty weapon to fight the dragons," he said,

digging the keychain out of his pants pocket and jangling a one-inch replica of a Colt Peacemaker.

"A twenty-mule team might help, too," Luke joked as he carried Judy into the reception.

"One mule is more than enough for me."

He sped toward the Markum house; the tires skimmed the tops of the bumps, and the roostertail of dust was a quarter-mile long, only slowing to let the dust settle some before he pulled into the driveway.

He got out, and hollered, "Hello, the house."

Rita yanked open the door, and dashed back to her computer without even a glance.

"I'm done. Just let me attach this file and send it."

He stood in the doorway, arms folded over his chest, watching her work. She was amazingly organized and he knew in his heart that she was the perfect choice for Vice President of International Operations. Then again, she was also the perfect choice for a rancher's wife. After all, a rancher's wife had to be a business partner as well as a marriage partner. Same with a bullfighter's wife.

Dagnabit, the woman was just perfect. He waited, hoping to appear patient, but he wanted to grab her into a full-body embrace and kiss every inch of her body. She glanced up at him, her blue eyes accentuated by her teal maid-of-honor gown. When she bent over her laptop, his gaze went straight to her rounded cleavage.

Trouble stirred in his southern hemisphere.

She snapped the case closed and stood. "All done."

He wrapped his arms around her. "I've been wanting to do this all day." He lowered his lips to hers, tasting her cherry-flavored lips, his heart beating with hot satisfaction when her breath caught and she kissed him back.

"Later, cowboy," she muttered shoving him back and grabbing her long, blue gloves.

He hoped she meant that.

When they walked into the reception, Phyllis directed them

to the buffet. "Choke it down, kids. We're about ready for the champagne and cake."

They made the rounds, greeting the guests—he, as best man; Rita, as maid of honor.

"You clean up pretty well," a local rancher joked.

"Looks like you cut the winter crop off your chin, too."

Rita laughed, her eyes bright. "You give as good as you get, don't you."

"You know it, and the way you're keeping me in a fever, I can hardly wait until later."

She raised an eyebrow and flashed a smile. "Who knows what the night will bring?"

Escorting such a fine lady around the room inflated more than his ego, and he avoided gazing at the soft wisps of hair brushing the back of her neck, or the curve of her shapely hips, or the low-cut neckline barely covering the sweetest of breasts.

Phyllis clanked a spoon on a glass and the noise level slowly died down. "It's time to get on with things. Brody, Rita, get up here."

Brody placed his hand on Rita's back and together they squeezed through the crowd to the table Phyllis had set up. Judy and Luke held crystal champagne flutes—the rest of them had plastic. With only five bottles of champagne for fifty people, Phyllis had augmented the supply with a couple of cases of merlot from Carmela Vineyards and a keg of Budweiser.

"First, I'd like to thank Phyllis for laying out such a fine spread for us this evening." Brody waited for the applause to die down, then continued, "Today, we witnessed the marriage of two of the nicest people on the planet. Please join me in a toast to Luke and Judy Bonner." Turning to the couple, he raised his flute. "May you have a long and happy life together."

"Cheers!" rang out throughout the hall. He pulled Rita closer to him while they both took a drink.

Luke and Judy stepped forward and Luke lifted his glass. "I'd like to toast Brody, the greatest best man, and Rita, the finest daughter a couple could ever have as the maid of honor. May you both find happiness!"

"Here, here!"

Brody's smile faded and his gut tied in a knot when his mother walked through the door as if she belonged there.

"And may I extend my heartfelt congratulations to the bride and groom, as well as the wedding attendants." She smiled as someone handed her a plastic flute filled to the brim with merlot. "*Salut.*"

The room went silent, for a moment, then cheers rang out again.

Then laughter, when Socrates, Perseus, Beauty, and Guinevere crashed the party.

Chapter 11

Desperate times call for desperate measures. When I saw that high-falutin' woman emerge like a queen bee from her half-mile-long limousine, I knew trouble had blown in from the East. The dogs and I had a little pow-wow and we decided she could only be Mrs. Pettybottham, come to collect our Rita.

We're not about to let her go without a fight. Whether she's aware enough to know it or not, she belongs with us—I felt so pampered while she was grooming me—and we've all agreed she does love Brody. We've made such headway, too! You've seen the calf-eyes those two have for one another.

But all our hard work will be for naught if this woman sticks her nose in our business.

Next mission: get rid of Mrs. Pettybottham and clear the way for romance.

Besides, I always did like a good party.

Brody's mother headed straight for him, much to his dismay. With one sentence, she could destroy his bullfighting career as well as the life he'd built with the goodhearted, hardworking people here in Grasmere.

And she'd do it.

At the last second, she veered to his right and offered her hand to Rita. "I'm Adelaide Pettybottham. You must be Rita Markum."

Rita's eyes widened and she paled a bit, but Brody was proud of the way she held her composure. "I am." She shook his mother's hand. "Nice to meet you, Mrs. Pettybottham." Tugging slightly on his arm, she said, "This is my neighbor, Brody Alexander."

He sent his mother a quick nod. Naturally, she smiled graciously, shooting him a warning with her gaze. He shot one right back.

Rita gestured toward Luke and Judy. "And this is my mom and her new husband, Judy and Luke Bonner."

Desperately trying to think of a way to get rid of her, Brody groaned when Phyllis started the wedding cake cutting ritual. At least his mother couldn't do anything disastrous for a few minutes. The worst thing was, Rita left his side and joined his mother, offering her a plate at the buffet.

But then, of course, there were the animals. Socrates headed straight for the beer and Brody dashed in front of the keg to head him off.

"No beer for you today, you alkie." Socrates leaned into Brody's sore ribs. "And cut that out."

The little mule let out a squeaky bray of protest, then, despite Brody's grab for his halter, trotted straight to their Unwelcome Guest. Before he could grab Socrates' collar, the mule had wrapped his lips over the top of her plastic champagne flute and upended it, hardly spilling a drop.

Brody managed to catch the flute and get a firm hold of the halter. He nearly laughed out loud—it was the first time in recorded history that he'd seen his mother speechless. He hoped she stayed that way until he could get her in the car and back on the road to the airport. "I think you'd better leave," he told her in a low voice as he led Socrates past her.

He scowled as a boy fed Perseus a hunk of Jell-O salad. Both dogs were making quite a killing in the scraps department—Perseus showing off his tricks, and Beauty staring at people with her sad bloodhound eyes. Doggy Tums would soon be in order.

Tying Socrates to the fender of his pickup, Brody went back in the house. He hoped he could get his mother out of there soon, but doubted she'd leave until she'd completed her agenda.

She stood by Rita, seemingly rapt in marvelous conversation. He should have known better, though. "So how did you meet this handsome young man?"

Rita smiled and clasped his hand. "I've known him since high school, when he moved to the ranch adjoining ours."

"So when's the wedding?"

Brody winced. Rita had made it clear that she'd never give up her corporate career, and in a way, he wouldn't want her to. It made her happy and more than anything, he wished her all the happiness in the world. He wished he fit in that world.

"Oh, we're not getting married—he has a ranch here and rodeos during the season. We're just good friends," Rita answered.

His mother smiled kindly, her eyes devious. He put his arm around Rita's shoulder and steered her toward Luke and Judy. "Your mom has a spot on her dress."

After he'd deposited her a safe distance away, he returned to his mother. Jaw tight, he asked, "What in the hell are you doing here?"

"You have papers to sign, Broderick, if you'll only quit rednecking long enough to read them. MOMMI can't run by itself. You'll either have to dissolve it, or find someone to run it. I'm not going to run Pettybottham Enterprises and MOMMI both."

"Come outside, so we can talk privately."

"It's dirty out there."

"Clean dirt—no grimy pavement."

"We'll talk in the car."

"We'll talk in the camper. I don't want anyone to see me in your car. Why the hell did you have to rent a stretch-limo?"

"A two-hour drive requires some creature comforts. But then," she scanned the room where his animals teased the guests, "you know all about creatures."

"If I sign the papers, will you leave?"

"Maybe, but I do find Miss Markum quite delightful—an excellent choice for a Pettybottham executive, I think."

"Very excellent." Which ruined his life, but excellent, nevertheless. He nudged his mother toward the door. "You have a date with the airlines to keep."

Judy thwarted him at the moat. "Mrs. Pettybottham, welcome! I hope you enjoy the reception. I know it doesn't have the whistles and bows you're used to, but the people here have warm hearts. The dancing will start momentarily."

"How kind," his mother said. "I'm quite embarrassed to appear at a wedding reception empty-handed, though."

"Nonsense," Judy said, steering his mother back into the fray. "We're glad to have you."

He followed closely behind the two women—for damage control. The band struck up a slow waltz. Luke took Judy in his arms for the first dance, and with her bum knee, they more rocked than danced, while gazing in each other's eyes.

"Such a touching scene," his mother whispered, "and they're probably honest with each other, too."

The pain in his side could have been his mother's barb, or the broken ribs as she patted him square on the injury.

"I'm staying until you consent to take your rightful place at Pettybottham Enterprises. Unless you want all these people to find out from me who you are, I suggest you humor me."

"Don't, Mother."

When the song ended, the bandleaders announced, "Brody and Rita will lead this one. The bride needs to set a spell."

"Behave yourself until we can talk," he hissed, then collected Rita for a slow two-step.

Rita worried her lower lip. "I wish I knew why Mrs. Pettybottham's here. Do you think she's had second thoughts about me? You know, country bumpkin and all?"

He pulled her closer, enjoying the feel of her breasts on his chest. "No, she's lucky to have you and I'm sure she's smart enough to know it." Not able to decide whether he wanted the dance to last forever with her in his arms, or for it to end quickly so he could get rid of his mother, he decided to enjoy the moment. He breathed in her lilac scent, knowing he'd think of her every time he smelled lilacs for the rest of his life.

And then it hit him square in the gut—he couldn't give her up. Not for the ranch, not for bullfighting, and not even for his animals.

Rita rested her cheek on Brody's shoulder. While not able to cast off the feeling that Mrs. Pettybottham studied her like a radar gun, she nestled in the security of his muscular arms wrapped around her as if he'd never let go.

"I don't know why she's here."

He brushed his hands over her back and pulled her closer. "I guess she couldn't wait to see what a wonderful person she promoted."

Lifting her head, she gazed into his eyes, nearly melting into their depths. "I doubt that."

He gently pushed her head back onto his shoulder. "Shhh, let's enjoy the dance."

And she did, thoroughly, breathing in the familiar but exhilarating scent of him—Old Spice, a bit of mule, and a tinge of alkali dust—knowing that within a few days, she'd rarely ever see him.

As the band struck the final chords, he pulled her to a back room and shut the door. "I love you, Rita."

He'd said it before, but this time his low voice caused her to get goosebumps all over. She smiled and hugged him tightly. "I know it, and you know that I love you. But this has only been a summer romance—I'm leaving in a few days."

"What would make you stay?"

Shrugging, she teased, "An executive position with a six-figure paycheck."

"Done. MOMMI needs an executive director and I have it on good authority that the benefactor is moving the head-quarters here."

"Ha ha. You're being ridiculous."

He nuzzled her neck. "Oh?"

"Yes. And I think I'd like to be on the Board of Directors of Pettybottham Enterprises, too."

"Done."

She giggled and pushed him back. "Get real, Brody."

"I'm as real as could be. At least I would be real if you agree to marry me." He got down on one knee and kissed her hand. "Will you be my wife?"

"No." She ran her fingers through her hair and turned her back to him. "Brody, you're making this so much worse. If I could, I would. Even being a cowboy's wife sounds good as long as that cowboy is you. But you have to understand, Luke isn't in all that good of shape, and Mom's going to need all the money I can make to get him through to old age."

"Luke's as healthy as I am. Besides, I can give you every one of the things I promised. I think you'd be a wonderful director for MOMMI." He turned her to face him and kissed her on the nose.

"Stop it!" She swatted lightly at him. "I seriously doubt Mrs. Pettybottham would agree."

"She doesn't need to." After closing his eyes and sighing, he opened them again before he dug out his wallet and showed her his driver's license. "I can give you anything you want. Yes, you can be the director of MOMMI. I formed the foundation with my inheritance. Ever wonder what it stands for? My Old Man's Money, Inc."

She read the name on the license. Broderick A. Pettybottham IV. The blood drained from her head and she leaned against the wall, slumping to the floor.

He knelt beside her. "I wanted to be a bullfighter—protect bullriders, entertain children. I wanted to fit in here, in Grasmere, and lift a beer with the local ranchers after feeding cattle in the snow. No one would ever believe that the majority owner of Pettybottham Enterprises could want that. They'd think I have ulterior motives." He brushed a whisper of hair from her cheek. "But after I came to know you even better, I fell in love with you, and I want you more than anything else."

He hugged her, but she pushed away from him and stood, stepping back, jaw tense, breath short. "So you lied to me and all these innocent people. You've been faking it for ten years. And now you want me to believe that you're suddenly an honest man?" She yanked open the door. "I'm firing myself."

She made her escape, running out the back, around the house and into her car. She tripped the locks as he ran up and pounded on the window. Without even casting a sideways glance at him, she started the engine, and peeled out, spraying gravel all over him and his camper. But who cared? He had plenty of money for a new paint job. Or hospital bills.

He'd played her for a fool. For over a third of her life she'd been obsessed with him, and the whole time he'd been toying with her.

"Most Eligible Bachelor of the Year, my ass," she hollered as she left the driveway. Tears streamed down her cheeks. She didn't even care.

"And Mrs. Pettybottham is my mother. I'm the majority owner and CEO of Pettybottham Enterprises." As Brody finished his confession, the party-goers remained silent. Their stunned faces made him feel all the more like a scoundrel. Socrates broke the tension by choosing that moment to clomp back in, chewed lead rope dangling.

Brody gave the mule a pat on the head, not having the heart to send the only friend he had away. Socrates stuck his nose inside Brody's tux jacket, and nibbled on his shirt pocket.

"Hell, you haven't fooled anyone besides yourself," Luke said, breaking the silence. "Whether you have more money than God or not, you're still a redneck at heart."

"Here, here!" his old friends yelled, followed by a mad rush to the keg.

One of the men, Larry, who'd helped build the children's

home raised his paper cup of suds and toasted, "Here's to the best gol-derned redneck bullfighter I know." The people cheered. "And the toughest. How many bones is busted right now?" They all laughed, and Brody laughed with them.

If only Rita could do the same.

"Just what in blue blazes is this here Pettybottham outfit?" Larry asked. "Does it do anything useful?"

Everyone laughed, but puzzled, Brody didn't have an answer. Basically, they pushed papers and made loads of money, but he didn't want to say that.

His mother stepped forward. "Pettybottham Enterprises was established over a hundred years ago by Broderick's great-great grandfather. Originally, it was an oil company, but in the twenties, he began diversifying. In its present state, Pettybottham is a Houston-based parent company to several others, including Waterson Insurance in Seattle, where Rita Markum worked the last few years."

Amidst the skeptical looks, Larry raised his paper cup. "I'll drink to that."

Brody wanted to clear out of there and find Rita, but he knew he needed to stay for at least a while when a few of the men asked him when the gypsum board was due to be delivered. He engaged in some small talk until Luke and Judy took him aside.

"You better get your fanny to the Markum's," his foreman told him. "Phyllis came in and said that Rita had called, and she's planning to catch a plane out of here tonight."

"Enough said." He clapped his friend on the shoulder. "Try to keep Socrates out of trouble."

On the way out, Socrates nuzzled his shirt pocket again. "You want the wedding ring? Sorry, boy, I couldn't tell you where it is. Wish I had it, though." He sighed. "I'll need all the help I can get."

In the pickup, he loosened his tie, and headed for Rita at break-neck speed.

As he turned onto the lane to her house, he glanced in the

rearview mirror and saw a dozen or more cars and pickups keeping pace with him—with a stretch-limo bottoming out, eating dust at the rear.

Nothing like making a dang fool of yourself in front of an audience. But it would be a small price to pay.

Rita jammed clothes in her suitcase willy-nilly. Unable to close it, she threw it on the floor and jumped on it, popping the hinges. "Take that, Broderick Alexander Pettybottham the Fourth!" She kicked the bag across the room and hopped across the floor holding her stubbed toe.

"I'd like to punch you right in the kisser!" Stuffing her toothbrush and a set of underwear in her overnight case, she decided to leave her clothes there. Her business wardrobe was still in Seattle, anyway.

She plopped on the bed, bouncing hangers all over the floor, and let loose a right jab into the pillow. "Right square in your drop-dead handsome kisser." Tears came again, making her even more angry.

Her stomach knotted at the sound of someone rapping at the door. Maybe she wouldn't answer it—only one person would follow her and he was the last person she wanted to see. Ever.

But neither did her mama raise a coward. She ran to the bathroom and splashed cold water on her face. He pounded again. With a glance in the mirror, she made a quick spit removal of the mascara on her cheeks.

She yanked the door open. Brody stood there, dust on his tux and a hang-dog expression. Which he deserved to have.

"What. Do. You. Want?" She breathed deep to prevent breaking into sobs again.

"You. Any way I can have you."

Several cars pulled into the driveway, kicking up dust.

She slammed the door, but he banged it back open before it could latch.

"Go away, Brody—or *Broderick*. Or maybe I should've

been calling you Mr. Pettybottham the Fourth all this time."

"I don't care what you call me, but I'm here to stay—at least, until you agree to marry me. Then I'll go anywhere you want me to, as long as it's with you."

"NO."

"Marry him, Rita!" A crowd had gathered behind him. Mortified, she tried to slam the door again, but this time he stepped halfway in, the corner of the door catching him in the ribs. Pain flickered across his face.

"Say *yes*, Rita." His jaw was tense and his eyes reflected her own yearning. "Give me your terms if you want to negotiate. You want me to play CEO at Pettybottham Enterprises, I'll do that. You want me to quit rodeoing, I'll do that. You want me to burn my house down, consider it done."

"*NO*." But she wanted him, she really did.

The people behind him booed, then chanted. "Say yes, say yes, say yes."

"I'm going to Seattle to look for a job. Without you."

She tried to slam the door, but he pushed into the house, closing the door behind him. "I love you. You love me. I already told you I'll give you anything you want."

"Except honesty, and that's the *only* thing I want."

"Honesty, too. I've told you everything."

She jabbed her forefinger in his chest. "So tell me, *Broderick*, how long would it have taken for you to get honest if your mother hadn't shown up, huh?" Jamming her hands on her hips, she glared at him.

"After the reception. I'd planned to come clean then."

"And Santa Claus wears a blue suit. How gullible do you think I am?"

The door opened and Socrates pushed his way in, followed by Perseus, Beauty, and Guinevere. Outside, the people still chanted, "Say yes, say yes."

Socrates turned sideways, leaning against Brody, shoving him against Rita, and knocking them both over. Perseus dropped something on her cheek.

"The ring," Brody murmured. "While I have you down,"—
he paused to nibble on her earlobe—"I might as well put this
ring on your finger."

She nearly melted as his warmth enveloped her. Fighting
against her weakening defenses, she struggled to roll from
under him, but Perseus sat on one side of her, Beauty plopped
her behind on the other, and Socrates stood over the top of
them. Guinevere propped her front paws on Rita's forehead and
glared at her.

"I amend that," Brody said. "Will you marry us?"

"Say yes, say yes," now accompanied by a clapping
cadence, much louder now, and she saw all her old friends
crammed into the kitchen.

Mrs. Pettybottham stepped forward. "Rita, I have to say that
I'm responsible for my son's deception, at least, in part. I
realize it's time for me to acknowledge that my little boy has
grown up, and that his life style is for him to choose."

Judy hobbled to the front of the crowd. "Forget anything I
ever said about never marrying a cowboy. You have to marry
the man of your heart, no matter what his profession is. But if
you expect him to support your dreams, then you have to
encourage him to follow his star, too."

Rita wondered why everyone had suddenly turned into a
bunch of philosophers. Must have been the merlot.

"So will you marry us?" Brody asked again.

She took a deep breath. It was hard to stay mad with a
handsome man on top of you and a skunk in your face. "I'll
think about it."

Chapter 12

I'm patient. More than patient. But now's the time for Rita to come to her right mind.

Actually, she wants to marry us—the radar in my ears can sense it. I was a little worried there for a minute, but I can see the question in her eyes and the flush on her cheeks.

Now all we have to do is make sure Brody doesn't screw everything up. I'm perched over the top of him, and I don't plan to move a muscle until he manages to get the correct answer from her. Yes, he's lifted me before—I don't weigh an ounce over three-hundred pounds—but I'm thinking he won't try it with those sore ribs of his.

Actually, I don't think he wants to. He's finally got Rita where he wants her. Underneath him.

You ever wonder about the silly positions that humans get in to mate? The rest of the animal kingdom just gets the job done, but humans can be downright ridiculous. I mean, what other animal would do it face-to-face, risking life and limb with the other's teeth. For that matter, this preoccupation with oral sex is a total bafflement. You'd never find another male animal that would willingly put his you-know-what in his mate's mouth. Not unless he didn't want it back. Ever.

But I'm off the subject. All we need is a single "yes," and we'll all be happy. And we plan to stay right where we are until that happens.

What's that you say, Perseus? No, you can't pee on a bush right now! We have work to do. Tie a knot in it.

And quit whining.

Perseus whimpered. Brody patted him on the head, then kissed Rita gently on the lips. "See, Perseus is begging, too."

Guinevere licked her on the cheek, and Beauty shoved her nose under Rita's left hand and lifted it up. Whimpering again, Perseus wiggled his behind even closer, under her left arm.

"Looks like the animals are ready for you to say yes."

He felt her relax under him. As for himself, his lower parts had put him in somewhat of an embarrassing position with the sexiest woman alive under him and a crowd watching him. That cross, however, he was plenty willing to bear. "So, Rita Markum, will you marry us?"

"Yes," she whispered.

He could hardly believe his ears. "What?"

"Yes, yes!" She kissed him full force. "But I don't want you to change a thing—except I do want a new house. And the first thing I'm going to do is burn those yellow curtains."

"Done."

The wedding guests cheered wildly, whistling and hollering. Socrates brayed and stepped away. Guinevere chattered, licking Rita's forehead. Perseus ran out of the room like a shot. Beauty ambled to Judy and lay down.

Brody thought his heart would burst with happiness. He kissed her full on the lips and slipped the ring on the fourth finger of her left hand.

She shoved against his chest. "Will you let me up now? This floor isn't getting any softer."

Brody stood and pulled his bride-to-be to her feet. He wrapped his arm around her waist, then turned to the best friends he ever could hope to have. "I'd like to announce that we're engaged to be married."

Several minutes of pandemonium lingered while the guests each congratulated the happy couple. When the room was finally empty, Rita, looking adorable with her hair pointing every which direction, said, "No matter what your name is, I love you with all my heart."

No two-thousand-pound bull had ever given him such weak knees.

Epilogue

It's a tough job, but someone has to do it. Babysitting, I mean. Why the heck was I hell-bent for leather to acquire Brodiettes? They're all over me, those ornery little creatures. And they have no respect whatsoever for my ears. Sigh.

I suppose you want an update. There are two Brodiettes. Cody is a three-year-old monster boy, cute as a button, but can't seem to hold still for a minute. I think we have another bullfighter on our hands. Our barrel racer's name is Moriah. She's five and is already training with an Appie named Parker. The horse spoils his human girl rotten. He and I've had words about that, to no avail.

Guinevere passed away in her sleep last year, but we still have Mrs. Pretty Bottom. No, Perseus still doesn't like her.

The man in the can, Brody has wisely decided to become a barrel man. He's getting up in the years to be in the cowboy protection business. We still do our act for the kids, though, and I enjoy it as much as ever.

But I like the winter best. Yes, it's cold, but the three-month hiatus from traveling is welcome. The kids settle in, and Perseus gets some much-needed rest. He's old for an Australian Shepherd, but you can't tell him that. He still insists on doing his old act, although Brody has shortened it some.

Best of all, I like to peer through the kitchen window while Brody and Rita make googly eyes at each other. After seven years of marriage they still do that.

And they have me to thank for it all.

181

Author Information

Jacquie Rogers is a former software designer, campaign manager, deli clerk, and cow milker, but always a bookworm. She lives in Seattle with her ever-patient husband and not-so-patient cat. Her hobbies include rodeo and fantasy baseball.

*Royalties from her first Highland Press release, **Faery Special Romances**, go to the Children's Tumor Foundation, ending neurofibromatosis through research.*

You're welcome to visit her website:
http://www.jacquierogers.com

Jacquie Rogers

Now Available:

Historicals:
                    Dawn Thompson
                    Rape of the Soul
                    Cindy Breeding
                    Fate of Camelot
                    Ashley Kath-Bilsky
                    The Sense of Honor
                    Isabel Mere
                    Almost Taken
                    Isabel Mere
                    Almost Guilty
                    Leanne Burroughs
                    Highland Wishes
                    Leanne Burroughs
                    Her Highland Rogue
                    Jennifer Linforth
                    Madrigal
                    Chris Holmes
                    Blood on the Tartan
                    Jean Harrington
                    The Barefoot Queen
                    Brynn Chapman
                    Bride of Blackbeard
                    Diane Davis White
                    Moon of the Falling Leaves
                    Molly Zenk
                    Chasing Byron
                    Katherine Deauxville
                    The Crystal Heart
                    Cynthia Owens
                    In Sunshine or In Shadow
                    Jannine Corti Petska
                    Rebel Heart
                    Phyllis Campbell
                    Pretend I'm Yours

Christian/   *Judith Leigh*
Inspirational: When the Vow Breaks
Non-Fiction/
  Writer's Resource: *Rebecca Andrews*
                    The Millennium Phrase Book
Contemporary: *Jean Adams*
                    Beats a Wild Heart

185

Mystery/Comedic:	*Katherine Deauxville*
	Southern Fried Trouble
Action/Suspense:	*Eric Fullilove*
	The Zero Day Event
Romantic Suspense:	*Candace Gold*
	A Heated Romance
	Jo Webnar
	Saving Tampa
Young Adult:	*R.R. Smythe*
	Into the Woods
	Anne Kimberly
	Dark Well of Decision
Anthologies:	*Michèle Ann Young/Kimberly Ivey/*
	Billie Warren Chai
	Brides of the West
	Deborah MacGillivray
	Cat O'Nine Tales

Deborah MacGillivray/Rebecca Andrews/Billie Warren Chai/
Debi Farr/Patricia Frank/Diane Davis White
Love on a Harley
Zoe Archer/Amber Dawn Bell/Gerri Bowen/
Candace Gold/Patricia Howell/Kimberly Ivey/Lee Roland
No Law Against Love 2
Jacquie Rogers
Faery Special Romances
Holiday Romance Anthology
Christmas Wishes
Holiday Romance Anthology
Holiday in the Heart
Romance Anthology
No Law Against Love
Romance Anthology
Blue Moon Magic
Romance Anthology
Blue Moon Enchantment
Romance Anthology
Recipe for Love
Deborah MacGillivray/Leanne Burroughs/
Amy Blizzard/Gerri Bowen/Judith Leigh
Love Under the Mistletoe
Deborah MacGillivray/Leanne Burroughs/Rebecca Andrews/
Amber Dawn Bell/Erin E.M. Hatton/Patricia Howell/
Isabel Mere
Romance Upon A Midnight Clear

*Check our website frequently for
future releases.
www.highlandpress.org*

Jacquie Rogers

Praise for Highland Press Books!

THE CRYSTAL HEART by Katherine Deauxville brims with ribald humor and authentic historical detail. Enjoy!

~ Virginia Henley, NY Times bestselling author

* * *

RAPE OF THE SOUL – Dawn Thompson clearly shows just what an amazing talent she was by instantly giving you a dark, suspenseful tale of horror. She described the book as 'Anya Seton meets Stephen King' and that is a fair assessment of its style. I would also say she added a touch of Daphne du Maurier and Arthur Quiller-Couch. Rape of the Soul is one of those books that will linger on bookshelves, and be read again and again.

Thompson delivers on all levels. When Jean Maitland enters the abandoned glass house of Craigmoor, you have a Hitchcock style, 'dark at the top of the stairs' foreboding that pure evil can exist and can reach from the past to destroy the future. Thompson delivers with this spellbinding tour de force, her legacy to her fans. It's a keeper.

~ PRN Reviews

* * *

THE SENSE OF HONOR - Ashley Kath-Bilsky has written a historical romance of the highest caliber. This reviewer fell in love with the hero and was cheering for the heroine all the way through. The characters are multi-dimensional and the secondary characters bring life to the story. Sexual tension rages through this story and Ms. Kath-Bilsky gives her readers a breath-taking romance. This reviewer was very pleased with how the author handled all the secrets. Sometimes it can be very frustrating for the reader when secrets keep tearing the main characters apart, but in this case, those secrets seem to bring them more together and both characters reacted very maturely when the secrets finally came to light. This reviewer is hoping that this very talented author will have another book out very soon.

~ Valerie, Love Romances

* * *

HIGHLAND WISHES by Leanne Burroughs. This reviewer found that this book was a wonderful story set in a time when tension was high between England and Scotland. The reader can feel this author's love for Scotland and its many wonderful heroes.

This reviewer was easily captivated by the story and was enthralled by it until the end. The reader will laugh and cry as you read this wonderful story. The reader feels all the pain, torment and disillusionment felt by both main characters, but also the joy and love they felt. Ms. Burroughs has crafted a well-researched story that gives a glimpse into Scotland during a time when there was upheaval and war for independence. This reviewer is anxiously awaiting her next novel in this series and commends her for a wonderful job done.

~Dawn Roberto, Love Romances

* * *

I adore this Scottish historical romance! **BLOOD ON THE TARTAN** by Chris Holmes has more history than some historical romances—but never dry history in this book! Readers will find themselves completely immersed in the scene, the history and the characters. Chris Holmes creates a multi-dimensional theme of justice in his depiction of all the nuances and forces at work from the laird down to the land tenants. This intricate historical detail emanates from the story itself, heightening the suspense and the reader's understanding of the history in a vivid manner as if it were current and present. The extra historical detail just makes their life stories more memorable and lasting because the emotions were grounded in events. The ending is quite special and bridges links with Catherine's mother's story as well as opening up this romance to an expansive view of Scottish history and ancestry. **Blood On The Tartan** is a must read for romance and historical fiction lovers of Scottish heritage.

~Merri, Merrimon Reviews

* * *

I can't say enough good things about Ms. Zenk's writing. **CHASING BYRON** by Molly Zenk is a page turner of a book not only because of the engaging characters but also by the lovely prose. In fact, I read the entire thing in one day. Reading this book was a jolly fun time all through the eyes of Miss Woodhouse, yet also one that touches the heart. It was an experience I would definitely repeat. I'm almost jealous of Ms. Zenk. She must have had a glorious time penning this story. As this is her debut novel, I hope we will be delighted with more stories from this talented author in the future.

~Orange Blossom, Long and Short Reviews

* * *

MOON OF THE FALLING LEAVES is an incredible read. The characters are not only believable, but the blending in of how Swift Eagle shows Jessica and her children the acts of survival is remarkably done. The months of travel indeed shows hardships each much endure. Diane Davis White pens a poignant tale that really grabbed this reader. She tells a descriptive story of discipline, trust and love in a time where hatred and prejudice abounded among many. This rich tale offers vivid imagery of the beautiful scenery and landscape, and brings in the tribal customs of each person, as Jessica and Swift Eagle search their heart.

~Cherokee, Reviewer for Coffee Time Romance

* * *

Jean Harrington's **THE BAREFOOT QUEEN** is a superb historical with a lushly painted setting. I adored Grace for her courage and the cleverness with which she sets out to make Owen see her love for him. The bond between Grace and Owen is tenderly portrayed and their love had me rooting for them right up until the last page. Ms. Harrington's **The Barefoot Queen** is a treasure in the historical romance genre you'll want to read for yourself! Five Star Pick of the Week!!!

~ Crave More Romance

* * *

IN SUNSHINE OR IN SHADOW by Cynthia Owens - If you adore the stormy heroes of 'Wuthering Heights' and 'Jane Eyre' (and who doesn't?) you'll be entranced by Owens' passionate story of Ireland after the Great Famine, and David Burke - a man from America with a hidden past and a secret name. Only one woman, the fiery, luscious Siobhan, can unlock the bonds that imprison him. Highly recommended for those who love classic romance and an action-packed story.

~ Best Selling Author, Maggie Davis,
AKA Katherine Deauxville

* * *

ALMOST TAKEN by Isabel Mere is a very passionate historical romance that takes the reader on an exciting adventure. Readers will watch in interest as Deran Morissey, the Earl of Atherton, and Ava Fychon, a young woman from Wales fall in love and overcome obstacles. This is a very sensual romance that wins the heart of the readers. The character's personalities will fascinate readers and win their concern. Ava, who is highly spirited and stubborn, will win the respect of the readers for her courage and determination. Deran, who is rumored in the beginning to be an ice king, not caring about anyone, will prove how wrong people's perceptions can be. ***Almost Taken*** by Isabel Mere is an emotionally moving historical romance that I highly recommend to the readers.

~ Anita, The Romance Studio

* * *

Leanne Burroughs easily will captivate the reader with intricate details, a mystery that ensnares the reader and characters that will touch their hearts. By the end of the first chapter, this reviewer was enthralled with ***HER HIGHLAND ROGUE*** and was rooting for Duncan and Catherine to admit their love. Laughter, tears and love shine through this wonderful novel. This reviewer was amazed at Ms. Burroughs' depth and perception in this storyline. Her wonderful way with words plays itself through each page like a lyrical note and will captivate the reader till the very end. Read ***Her Highland Rogue*** and be transported to a time that is full of mystery and promise of a future. This reviewer is highly recommending this book for those who enjoy an engrossing Scottish tale full of humor, love and laughter.

~ Dawn Roberto, Love Romances

* * *

PRETEND I'M YOURS by Phyllis Campbell is an exceptional masterpiece. This lovely story is so rich in detail and personalities that it just leaps out and grabs hold of the reader. Ms. Campbell carries the reader into a mirage of mystery with deceit, betrayal of the worst kind, and a passionate love that makes this a whirlwind page-turner. Mercedes and William are astonishing characters that ignite the pages and allows the reader to experience all their deepening sensations. This extraordinary read had me mesmerized with its ambiance, its characters and its remarkable twists and turns, making it one recommended read in my book.

~ Linda L., Fallen Angel Reviews

* * *

REBEL HEART by Jannine Corti Petska - Ms. Petska does an excellent job of all aspects of sharing this book with us. Ms. Petska used a myriad of emotions to tell this story and the reader quickly becomes entranced in the ways Courtney's stubborn attitude works to her advantage in surviving this disastrous beginning to her new life. This is a wonderful rendition of a different type which is a welcome addition to the historical romance genre. I believe that you will enjoy this story; I know I did!

~ Brenda Talley, The Romance Studio

* * *

SOUTHERN FRIED TROUBLE - Katherine Deauxville is at the top of her form with mayhem, sizzle and murder.

~ Nan Ryan, NY Times bestselling author

* * *

INTO THE WOODS by R.R. Smythe - This Young Adult Fantasy will send chills down your spine. I followed Callum and witnessed everything he and his friends went through as they attempted to decipher the messages. At the same time, I watched Callum's mother, Ellsbeth, as she walked through the Netherwood. Each time Callum deciphered one of the four messages, some villagers awakened. Through the eyes of

Ellsbeth, I saw the other sleepers wander, make mistakes, and be released from the Netherwood, leaving Ellsbeth alone. There is one thread left dangling, but do not fret. This IS a stand-alone book. But that thread gives me hope that another book about the Netherwoods may someday come to pass. Excellent reading for any age of fantasy fans!
~ Detra Fitch, Huntress Reviews

* * *

BRIDES OF THE WEST by Michèle Ann Young, Kimberly Ivey, and Billie Warren Chai - All three of the stories in this wonderful anthology are based on women who gambled their future in blindly accepting complete strangers for husbands. It was a different era when a woman must have a husband to survive and all three of these phenomenal authors wrote exceptional stories featuring fascinating and gutsy heroines and the men who loved them. For an engrossing read with splendid original stories I highly encourage reader's to pick up a copy of this marvelous anthology.
~ Marilyn Rondeau, Reviewers International Organization

* * *

CAT O'NINE TALES by Deborah MacGillivray. Enchanting tales from the most wicked, award-winning author today. Spellbinding! A treat for all.
~ Detra Fitch, Huntress Reviews

* * *

FAERY SPECIAL ROMANCES - Brilliantly magical! Ms. Rogers' special brand of humor and imagination will have you believing in faeries from page one. Absolutely enchanting!
~ Dawn Thompson, Award Winning Author

* * *

Christmas is a magical time and twelve talented authors answer the question of what happens when **CHRISTMAS WISHES** come true in this incredible anthology. **Christmas Wishes** shows just how phenomenal a themed anthology can be. Each of these highly skilled authors brings a slightly different perspective to the Christmas theme to create a book that is sure to leave readers satisfied. What a joy to read such splendid stories! This reviewer looks forward to more anthologies by Highland Press as the quality is simply astonishing.
~ Debbie, CK2S Kwips and Kritiques

* * *

RECIPE FOR LOVE - I don't think the reader will find a better compilation of mouth watering short romantic love stories than in **Recipe for Love**! This is a highly recommended volume–perfect for beaches, doctor's offices, or anywhere you've a few minutes to read.
~ Marilyn Rondeau, Reviewers International Organization

* * *

HOLIDAY IN THE HEART - Twelve stories that would put even Scrooge into the Christmas spirit. It does not matter what *type* of romance genre you prefer. This book has a little bit of everything. The stories are set in the U.S.A. and Europe. Some take place in the past, some in the present, and one story takes place in both! I strongly suggest that you put on something comfortable, brew up something hot (tea, coffee or cocoa will do), light up a fire, settle down somewhere quiet and begin reading this anthology.
~ Detra Fitch, Huntress Reviews

* * *

BLUE MOON MAGIC is an enchanting collection of short stories. You should have no problem finding a tale to suit your mood. **Blue Moon Magic** offers historicals, contemporaries, time travel, paranormal, and futuristic narratives to tempt your heart.

Legend says that if you wish with all your heart upon the rare blue moon, your wishes were sure to come true. True love is out there if you just believe in it. In some of the stories, love happens in the most unusual ways. Angels may help, ancient spells may be broken, anything can happen. Even vampires will find their perfect mate with the power of the blue moon. Not every heroine believes they are wishing for love, some are just looking for answers to their problems or nagging questions.

Blue Moon Magic is a perfect read for late at night or even during your commute to work. The short yet sweet stories are a wonderful way to spend a few minutes. If you do not have the time to finish a full-length novel, but hate stopping in the middle of a loving tale, I highly recommend grabbing this book.

~ Kim Swiderski, Writers Unlimited Reviewer

* * *

Legend has it that a blue moon is enchanted. What happens when fifteen talented authors utilize this theme to create enthralling stories of love?

BLUE MOON ENCHANTMENT is a wonderful, themed anthology filled with phenomenal stories by fifteen extraordinarily talented authors. Readers will find a wide variety of time periods and styles showcased in this superb anthology. **Blue Moon Enchantment** is sure to offer a little bit of something for everyone!

~ Debbie, CK²S Kwips and Kritiques

* * *

NO LAW AGAINST LOVE - If you have ever found yourself rolling your eyes at some of the more stupid laws, then you are going to adore this novel. Each story deals with at least one stupid or outdated law. Let me give you an example: In Florida, USA, there is a law that states 'If an elephant is left tied to a parking meter, the parking fee has to be paid just as it would for a vehicle.' No matter how many times you go back and reread them, the words will remain the same. The tales vary in time and place. Some take place in the present, in the past, in the USA, in England...in other words, there is something for everyone! Best yet, profits from the sales of this novel will go to breast cancer prevention.

A stellar anthology that had me laughing, sighing in pleasure, believing in magic, and left me begging for more! Will there be a second anthology someday? I sure hope so! This is one novel that will go directly to my 'Keeper' shelf, to be read over and over again. Very highly recommended!

~ Detra Fitch, Huntress Reviews

* * *

LOVE UNDER THE MISTLETOE is a fun anthology that infuses the beauty of the season with fun characters and unforgettable situations. This is one of those books that you can read year round and still derive great pleasure from each of the charming stories. A wonderful compilation of holiday stories. Perfect year round!

~ Chrissy Dionne, Romance Junkies

Jacquie Rogers

Highland Press

Assorted Lines

☐ 9780974624990 Faery Special Romances $13.45
☐ 9780978713904 Cat O' Nine Tales $12.49
☐ 9780980035605 Moon of the Falling Leaves $12.49

Highland Press, PO Box 2292, High Springs, FL 32655

www.highlandpress.org

Please send me the books I have checked above. I am enclosing $_____(Please add $2.50 per book to cover shipping and handling). Send check or money order—no C.O.D.s please. Or, PayPal – Leanne@leanneburroughs.com and indicate names of book(s) ordered.

Name_____

Address_____

City_____State/Zip_____

Please allow 2 weeks for delivery. Offer good in US only. (Contact
The.Highland.Press@gmail.com for shipping charges outside the US.)

Breinigsville, PA USA
22 June 2010
240417BV00001B/168/P